HOTTEST
SUMMER
EVER

JIMMY DASAINT
TIONA BROWN

HOTTEST SUMMER EVER

Published by DASAINT ENTERTAINMENT
Po Box 97 Bala Cynwyd, PA 19004
Website: www.dasaintentertainment.com

Every single person wants to be loved

They'll search their entire life, beyond the mighty skies above

They'll hope and pray for this love to soon appear

But often love confuses the mind and rarely does it play fair

It comes and goes, and even plays lots of games

Bringing pain and joy and never leaving anyone feeling the same

Still, everyone will follow love- until their death

Experiencing all of its emotions before we take our final breath

From the young and naïve to the old, wise, and gray

We will continue to chase love until it stops running **away.**

Jimmy DaSaint

Charm is deceitful, and beauty is passing,
But a woman who fears the Lord, she shall be praised.

Proverbs 31:30

June 29, 1987

"Come here, sweetie," Sonny said, calling his five-year-old daughter Summer. Running and jumping up into her father's arms, Summer gave him a big loving hug. "Daddy!"

"Did you have fun with your Aunt Helen and Uncle Dwight?" her loving father asked. "Yes, Daddy. Uncle Dwight took me to the park. I rode on the swings and the sliding board. And Aunty Helen took me to McDonalds," Summer excitedly said. "Okay, sweetie, go get in the car. I'll be right there in a minute," Sonny said, walking over to Helen and Dwight.

Summer rushed inside of Sonny's running white Cadillac, and shut the door and waited for her father.

"Thanks for babysitting, Y'all, I really appreciate it. I don't know what I would do without you two," Sonny said wholeheartedly. "Oh, we enjoyed it, Sonny. Summer is a sweet child. She's never a problem at all," Helen said. "Yeah, buddy, I told you if you ever need a babysitter just to drop her off and Helen and I will look after her. But next time just try and let us know if you'll be gone for more than a day," Dwight smilingly said, giving Sonny a playful push.

"I'm sorry about that. It won't happen again. I just had to handle some important business," Sonny replied. "It's not a problem, Sonny. We truly enjoyed Summer's company," Dwight said.

After giving Helen a hug and shaking Dwight's hand, Sonny got back into his Cadillac where Summer was inside waiting.

"Bye, bye, Aunt Helen and Uncle Dwight," Summer yelled out the window, waving her little arms. After waving goodbye, Helen and Dwight went back into their house.

"Put on your seatbelt, sweetie," Sonny said, pulling off down the street. "Okay, Daddy," Summer said, strapping herself in the seatbelt. "You miss Daddy?" Sonny asked, rubbing his hands through her long black hair. "Yes, Daddy, I missed you so much. Are you gonna go away again?" Summer asked, in a saddened tone.

"No, Daddy's not going anywhere," Sonny said, smiling. "It's all you and me now," he said convincingly. "You promise me, Daddy?" Summer said, with her sweet, innocent little voice. "I promise you, Summer. Daddy will never, ever leave you again. Do you remember what I told you?" her father asked.

"Yeah, I remember, Daddy," Summer said softly. "And what's that?" Sonny said, turning down his car radio. "That you will never leave me alone, and no man can love me more than you can," Summer said proudly. "And what else?" Sonny asked as he continued to drive down the street with a big smile on his face.

"If a man can't love me just like you, then he ain't worth being with at all," Summer said, as her enormous smile covered her tiny face.

CHAPTER 1
May 16, 2005

Prince

As she walked gracefully across the crowded street, I couldn't help but stare out of my car window at the fine female specimen that was in front of me. Immediately I found an empty parking space and parked my car. Watching her walk into a neighborhood hair salon, I quickly followed behind her. As I walked inside, the well-decorated salon was filled with attractive young women all waiting for their weekly hair appointments. Looking around, I didn't see the beautiful female whom I had run in after.

"Are you looking for someone?" a lovely voice said, coming from behind me. As I turned around to see who it was, a smile came upon my face.

"Yeah, I was looking for you," I said, staring into her beautiful brown eyes. "Me? Do you have an appointment today?" she asked, looking on the notepad she held in her hands. "No, I don't have an appointment. I saw you when I was driving, so I parked and followed you in here."

"All of that for little ole me?" she smiled, showing her perfect white teeth. "Yeah, all that for little ole you," I said, as my eyes started moving up and down, completely checking her out.

"Oh, I'm just making sure you didn't park that pretty blue Mercedes-Benz for anybody else up in here," she said, smiling. "So you saw me?" I asked, now shocked and a little embarrassed.

"From a mile away, handsome," she said, folding her arms across her chest. "What's your name," I asked her trying to rebuild my confidence. "My name is Summer. Summer Jones," she said captivatingly. "Summer," I said grinning because she said it so cute. "Yeah, like the opposite of winter," she jokingly responded. "And what's yours?" she asked, waiting for an answer. "My name is Prince. And since we are using full names, then it's Prince Love, but everyone just calls me Prince."

"Prince Love," she grinned. "Love, huh?"
"Yeah, Love, like the opposite of hate," I jokingly said.
"So how can I help you, Love, I mean Prince?"
"I'ma be straight up with you, Summer. When I saw you walking across the street, my heart felt like it stopped beating inside my chest. I don't want you to think that this is some type of game that I'm playing, or that this is something that I do all the time. Believe me; it's not. But the moment I saw you, Summer, something told me just to follow my instincts and run in here after you."

"Why me?" Summer blushingly said, laying the appointment pad down on the counter. "Because you are the second most beautiful woman that I've ever laid my eyes on. That's why."
"And who's the first?" Summer said, waiting for an immediate answer. "My mother. She passed away a while ago. But she'll always be the most beautiful woman ever to me."

"Oh, that is so cute," Summer said, shaking her head and seeing my sincerity. "I also lost my mother. She died when I was only four years old."

"My sincere condolences. I'm sorry to hear that. So do you have a boyfriend or a husband?" I said, changing the sensitive subject.

"No, I don't have a husband," Summer playfully frowned.

"What about a boyfriend?" I asked.

"Well, I had a boyfriend, but he's gone."

"Oh, I'm sorry. He died?"

"No, he was just sent to prison for three years."

"How long has he been in?" I asked, shaking my head as if I cared.

"What time is it?" Summer asked me. Looking at my 18 karat gold Movado watch, "Its 2:15," I said.

"He's been locked up for two hours."

"Two hours! Stop it!"

"Yup, I just left the courthouse downtown. He was just sentenced to serve thirty-six months in a state prison."

"Are you serious?"

"Dead serious. But it's been over, though. I was just showing my support as a good friend. We had plenty of problems way before he caught his case. And he knew it was over."

"You mind if I ask you what he's in prison for?"

"Drugs! Selling drugs on a street corner with his stupid friends. I told him a thousand times that sooner or later the law would catch up with him, but Malcolm never listened to me."

"So his name is Malcolm?"

"Yeah, that's his name, but I don't want to talk about him," she said showing her lack of concern for him. "Cool with me. So are you busy tonight, Ms. Jones?" I said, getting straight to the point.

"Are you asking me out, Mr. Love?" she retorted smiling.

"You can't answer a question with a question," I said.

"I just did, handsome."

"Well, yes, I am asking you out, Summer."

"Then, no, I'm not busy tonight. I close up around nine. You can pick me up here at the salon."

"Where's your boss. I'll pay them your whole day's salary if they let you leave right now," I said, looking around the salon full of nosy people.

"You're talking to the boss," Summer said.

"Excuse me! My bad. So this is your hair salon?"

"It's been all mine for two years now. I see you didn't look at the large sign that's out front."

"I guess I missed it, but I'll make sure I take a peek at it on my way out. I'll let you get back to work, Summer, but I'll be back at nine on the dot," I said, preparing myself to walk away from this breathtaking beauty.

"I won't have to bring my mace, will I?"

"If you thought you did, I don't think you would be letting me take you out," I quickly answered.

"Okay, handsome, nine o'clock then. I'll be waiting for you out front," she smiled. "Alright, Summer, I'll see you later." As I walked away, I could feel her eyes following me out the door.

~~~

"Who was that?" the tall, attractive deep brown-skinned female said, walking up to Summer.

"Some guy I just met. His name is Prince."

"He's a cutie! Damn, does he have a brother?"

"I don't know, Keisha. He didn't say."

"Well do me a favor and find out," Keisha said, playfully pushing Summer's shoulder.

"Girl, don't you have a man already?"

"So what! I'm sure he's out getting some ass from someone else, so why can't I find me a secret lover?" Keisha said, laughing.

"You better not let Boo find out. You know what happened the last time he caught you creeping," Summer said, walking towards the back room.

Prince

Outside, I looked up at the large advertisement out front of the hair salon. "Summer's Unisex Hair Salon," it read in large bold black letters. All of the times that I had driven down 48th Street, I had never noticed the sign until today.

~~~

Summer's hair salon was located on the west side of Philadelphia. The large three-story building where she operated and ran her hair salon from the first floor was on the corner of 48th and Woodland Avenue. Right above the hair salon were two small apartments that Summer rented out. The property was given to Summer by her father, Sonny, who owned a few other properties, a barbershop and a bar just a couple blocks away from Summer's hair salon.

Sonny was well respected throughout the community, and he was a very over-protective father of his only child, Summer. There wasn't too much around this small congested neighborhood that Sonny didn't know about. His barbershop was where everyone who was anyone would come to get haircuts and talk about what was happening on the streets. From the good to the bad, Sonny knew it all.

Prince

After getting into my car, I started the engine and pulled out from my parking space. As I slowly drove away, I couldn't help but think about the beautiful woman that I just met. It was truly a challenge to get this girl out of my thoughts.

Summer stood around 5'5" in height with a light honey brown complexion, and she had dark black average length hair. Her full lips and high cheekbones brought out her exotic features. Though she was much younger than I had expected, she was someone that I was looking forward to getting to know. I wasn't about to let the fact that she was twenty-three stop me from making a connection with her. Summer appeared very mature and well-rounded despite her age.

Once I finished doing my daily routines, I drove back home to get myself ready for my date. It was only a few hours away, and I anticipated seeing Summer's gorgeous face again. After taking a soothing warm shower, I got dressed, went into the living room, sat back and watched some television on my new Sony flat screen.

As I watched an old Mike Tyson fight on E.S.P.N, I still couldn't help but think about the gorgeous and intriguing Ms. Summer Jones.

8:58 P.M.

"Keisha, make sure you and Latoya straighten things up before you lock up the shop tonight," Summer said, fixing her hair in front of the large mirror. "Don't we always?" Keisha said, with a sarcastic glare on her face. "Just make sure you lock up, girl. Damn, you always got something smart to say."

"Okay, boss, I'll take care of everything," Keisha jokingly said. "Now was that all that hard?" Summer said, walking over to the window and looking outside. "Where is he taking you?" Latoya asked. "I don't know, Latoya, he didn't say," Summer said, taking a seat in an empty styling chair. "Well, I hope you enjoy yourself, girl. Make sure you fill us in with all of the details in the morning," Latoya said, smiling. "Thanks, Toya," Summer said, looking at her Rolex Cellini watch.

Latoya and Keisha had both been Summer's two closest friends since elementary school. They also were hair stylists who had been working at the salon since its grand opening.

Latoya was a short, hippy, attractive dark-skinned woman with a very warm personality and she was outgoing in nature. She lived above the hair salon with her nine-year-old son, Nolan.

Keisha was much taller, standing around 5'9", thin, with a deep brown complexion and long, straight hair that hung just below her shoulders. Known for her gold-digging ways and sassy attitude, not only was Keisha attractive, but she took no shit from anyone. Every morning, Keisha would leave her North Philadelphia home and drive to work in her new, gold Acura TSX that her boyfriend, Boo, had bought for her. She always held her head high and felt she was the cat's meow.

"Your friend just pulled up, Summer," Keisha said, looking out the window at the dark blue Mercedes double parking out front of the shop. "Call me later," Latoya said. "Me, too," Keisha added. "Okay, I'll talk to y'all heffas later," Summer smilingly said, getting up from the chair and walking to the front door.

"Don't do anything that I wouldn't do," Keisha shouted. "Girl, who you fooling? You done it all," Latoya said, as they both started laughing. "Bye, girls," Summer said, shutting the door behind her.

Running to the window, Keisha and Latoya watched as Prince got out of the car to open the passenger side door for Summer. Quickly getting back inside of his car, he pulled off and drove down the street.

Prince

"I see that you're prompt," Summer said, looking at me as I drove. "Yes, always. You have to treat people the way you want to be treated," I replied. "What's that you're wearing? It smells good." Summer asked, inhaling the warm scent of my cologne. "It's called Intuition. You like it?" "Yes, it smells so nice. So where are you taking me tonight?" "It's a surprise. You'll see when we get there," I said with a smile.

"So what type of music do you like, Prince?" "R&B, some light jazz, and old school hip hop. I'm not really into all the new rap. But I do like P. Diddy, Dre, and Jay-Z. Oh and Nelly ain't bad either."

"Do you mind telling me how old you are?"
"No, not at all. I'm thirty-three years young."
"Stop playing! Ain't no way!"
"I'm serious. I just turned thirty-three last month."
"You don't look a day over twenty-five."

"Well, I try to take care of myself. I don't smoke or drink, and I make sure I get to the gym a few times a week."

"Thirty-three!" Summer said, shaking her head.

"Why, am I too old for you?"

"No, I'm just shocked, that's all. You look so much younger."

"So what's the age of the oldest man that you've ever dated, Summer?"

"Twenty-four, and that was my ex-boyfriend, Malcolm."

"Don't worry; I don't bite," I said, looking over at the sexy smile on her face.

Hearing her cell phone ring, Summer opened up her Coach bag and took out her small phone. "Hello," she answered. "Yes...uh, huh...okay...I said okay. Love you too, bye, bye," Summer said, closing her cell phone and putting it back inside of her bag.

"Everything okay?" I said, stopping my car at a red light. "Yes. That was my father, just making sure I was alright. He called the shop, and my girlfriends told him that I had just left."

"Do you have any brothers and sisters, Summer?"

"Nope. I'm the only child. It's just me."

"So you're Daddy's little girl then?"

"Yup, Daddy's little girl," she smiled proudly. "What about you, Prince, do you have any siblings?"

"I have an older brother. He lives in Miami with his wife and kids. We aren't close, so we don't communicate much. Actually at all."

Hearing an R. Kelly song come on the radio, I turned up the volume a little. "Oh, that's my song," Summer said, as she began singing the chorus. "My body's callin for you. My body's callin for you." "So you like R. Kelly, huh?" I said as I started driving again. "I love his music. I have every one of his CDs at home. R. Kelly, Prince, Maxwell, Avant, Musiq, Jill Scott, Angie Stone. Anything that's neo-soul I probably have it. I love listening to music that has a meaning, and that's sexy." As she sat back enjoying the smooth ride, I just smiled and didn't say a word as she continued to sing along with the song.

Twenty minutes later I pulled my car into a large parking lot on Delaware Avenue with three huge helicopters. After I had parked my car, the two of us got out and approached a female inside a small ticket booth.

"Prince Love, I called and made reservations earlier today," I said, showing the woman my driver's license. "Mr. Love, you'll be riding in helicopter number two. The pilot is expecting you, sir," she said, pointing me in the right direction.

"Have you ever been on a helicopter ride, Summer?" "No, and I've only been on a plane once, and that was to go to the Bahamas with my two girlfriends."
"Well, just trust me. You're gonna enjoy it," I said, grabbing her left hand and walking up to the pilot. "Prince Love," I said, shaking his hand. "Welcome aboard, Mr. Love. Your seats are ready," he said.

As we climbed on board, a young white couple was already seated inside. After the pilot got in, he received the lift off signal from a male employee. Moments later, the large black helicopter rose off the ground. Still holding Summer's soft, well-manicured hand, we watched as the large steel bird began to fly through the air.

"Where are we going?"

"To dinner."

"Where at, Mars?" Summer sarcastically asked.

"No, in New York," I answered.

"New York? Are you serious?"

"Yes, the helicopter will land on top of the Salvatore Restaurant in Manhattan. We'll be escorted to our seats and promptly waited on. After dinner we'll get right back on the helicopter and the pilot will fly us back to Philadelphia."

"I see you're full of surprises."

"You ain't seen nothing yet, beautiful," I said with a big grin plastered on my face.

As the helicopter headed towards the Big Apple, we continued to watch the elegant night scenery as the Philadelphia skyline slowly disappeared.

That night, the two of us enjoyed a delicious lobster meal, as we talked and got to know each other a little better. Through our conversation, I found out that Summer was well educated. She had attended the top rated Catholic schools for twelve years of her academic life, and she also graduated from LaSalle University with a degree in Business Management. So not only was she drop-dead gorgeous but to me, she was even more beautiful because her brain wasn't filled with loads of emptiness. Her conversation was filled with substance, and I enjoyed being in her company.

After returning to Philly, I dropped Summer off at her hair salon. She gave me a soft kiss on my cheek before she got into her cherry red Lexus that was parked directly in front of her shop. Rolling down her window, she called me over to her car.

"Hey beautiful, what's up?" I said, walking back over to her car.

"I just wanted to tell you once again that I enjoyed myself. You were a true gentleman, and I really appreciate that," she said, as her beautiful smile lit up her canvas.

"Thank you, Summer. Will you be okay getting home?"

"Oh, I'll be fine. Don't you worry about me, handsome."

"Okay. But don't forget to call me and let me know you're home safe."

"I won't. I'll call you as soon as I get in the house. I promise. Bye, bye, Prince."

"Bye, Summer," I said, walking over to my car.

As I walked away, I could feel her eyes once again glued to my every move. "You like what you see?" I turned around and said with a smile. "I think you know the answer already," she said, rolling up her window and pulling off down the street.

Once she drove off, I got back into my car and drove off as well. Tonight I enjoyed myself, and I wished this memorable night didn't have to come to an end.

After Summer had called me to let me know she had gotten in the house safely, we continued to talk on the phone for a few hours. Each moment we shared on the phone I felt as if I was grower closer to her, and even with sleep filling my eyes I didn't want to hang up. When we did finally end the call, I laid back on my bed and thought about when I would see Summer's beautiful face again. I then closed my eyes and finally fell asleep with her image still shining in my mind.

CHAPTER 2

Summer

Early the next morning, Keisha, Latoya and I were inside the hair salon talking. I told my two girlfriends about the wonderful night I had with Prince. They found it hard to believe that I had just met this man, and our date was setup as if I was inside a fairytale or in a dream. I bragged about my evening because to date it had been the best date I'd ever been on. I also I told them how much I was looking forward to seeing Prince again. He had an important business meeting that he needed to attend in Washington, DC, so it would be a couple of days before I could see him again.

"How was the helicopter ride to New York?" Latoya asked. "I was a little scared at first, but then Prince put his arm around me, and everything just seemed so right. We held hands the whole ride up, and then even on the flight back to Philly," I blushed. "Sounds like you found your Prince Charming," Latoya said.

"I'ma just take it one day at a time. I'm still getting over Malcolm," I confessed. "Girl, Malcolm is so yesterday. It's about today and tomorrow. What woman wouldn't want a man like Prince? He's fine as hell, successful and smart, with no kids either. Malcolm who?" Keisha said, as we all burst out laughing. Keisha was too much; I thought to myself.

"But all jokes aside, Malcolm was my first. So I feel like I still gotta be there for him. Especially now since he's in jail. We are still good friends, and I don't want to turn my back on him completely." "She's right, Keisha, you can't just forget about your man or your ex-boyfriend just because he goes off to prison. That wouldn't be right," Latoya said, looking at Keisha shaking her head.

"To each his own. If a nigga can't do anything for me, then why should I break my neck for his ass? I got needs and bills to pay," Keisha said. "I'm just saying do you, but don't stop doing them either. A man can never truly forgive a woman who leaves him while he's in prison. Don't you have two older brothers that are locked up, Keisha? You should know already. Look at all the money orders you send them each month. They need family and friends the most during these times," Latoya said.

"She's right, Keisha. I would never run off on Malcolm. We had some good times. The least I could do is be his friend."

"Okay, I get the message," Keisha said, still unmoved.

"So where does Prince work?" Latoya asked.

"He's an out of state contractor for a real estate firm. They buy property in different states and sell them. He told me sometimes his job requires him to travel for days to get the deals handled."

"You sure he ain't got no wife and kids somewhere because he just seems too good to be true," Keisha said.

"Well, believe it 'cause it's all true. He's single with no kids, and if he does have a woman somewhere out there, I'm gonna make sure he forgets about her ass," I said sternly.

"That's right, girl, put your mark down," Latoya shouted.

"Well now that you have an older and more mature male friend, maybe you'll finally get to experience what it feels like to have an orgasm. Lord knows, you would have never found out if you stayed with Malcolm, Mr. Five-minute man," Keisha said. "Shut up, Keisha," I playfully said, as all three of us started laughing. "Leave my Malcolm alone. I shouldn't have ever told Y'all."

As the three of us were talking, I heard my cell phone ringing. Walking over to the counter where my phone was, I answered it.

"Hello, this is Summer."

"Hey, beautiful, it's me, Prince."

"Hey, I was just talking about you to my girlfriends."

"I hope it was all good."

"It was," I said, happy to hear his voice.

"I called to let you know that I've been thinking about you all morning."

"You have?"

"That's my word, all morning long you've been on my mind."

"Stop, you're making me blush."

"So did you think about me? Not just talk about me; have you been thinking about me?"

"Why ask me questions that you already know the answers to?"

"Just answer the question."

"Yes, Prince, I couldn't get you off my mind. And I didn't want to. Are you happy now?"

"I'm ecstatic. You've made my day, Summer. Listen, I'll be back in Philly tomorrow evening. Can I see you again, beautiful?"

"Hold on, let me check and see if it's cool with my home girls," I said, putting the phone down to my chest. "Keisha, Latoya, Prince wants to know if he could see me tomorrow,"

I yelled out. "Yeah, Prince," both my girls yelled back in unison.

"Did you hear that?" I said, speaking back into the phone. "Yes, I heard them loud and clear. I'll call you later tonight. I have to make a run and handle some business." "Bye, Prince. You can call me at my home number. I'll be there," I said calmly, not wanting to seem too desperate. "Alright, beautiful. I'll talk to you later," Prince said, hanging up.

After ending the call, I walked back to the front of the shop where Keisha and Latoya were waiting for me.

"Damn, girl, you need to take that big ass smile off your face," Keisha said, as she rinsed out a customer's hair. "You're just jealous."
"Yeah, stop hating, Keisha," Latoya said, smiling.
"Nope, not until I find me my Prince Charming," Keisha said as we all started laughing together once again.

For the rest of the day, Prince stayed on my mind. I couldn't wait until the shop closed so I could get home and hear his voice again. I didn't know what it was about this man, but whatever it was, it was already becoming addictive. I caught myself yearning and craving someone I didn't even know. Scary as it was, I wasn't afraid to get to know what this man was all about. And I wanted to know now.

Later That Evening
The group of young and old men were seated around the large barbershop talking. Sonny's barbershop was where everyone would come for some of the best conversation around. And the haircuts weren't bad either. The five

oversized black barber chairs were all being occupied by paying clients. There wasn't an empty customer's chair in site. A large vending machine stood next to the Coca Cola machine. Pictures and large mirrors covered the four white walls. A 48" Panasonic color television sat on a wooden shelf, along with a matching CD player and radio receiver. Over the top of the barbershop is where Sonny lived inside his plush two-bedroom apartment. But inside the large basement, a whole other world existed.

Three round crap tables along with slot machines and blackjack tables filled the huge basement. Thick black carpet covered the entire floor. A bar filled with top-shelf and well-known liquors, vodkas and wines had been built along the back wall. It had its own back entrance and every Friday, Saturday and Sunday night, the Basement, as it was known, would be filled with people. Old and young hustlers and gamblers, male and female, showed up faithfully to win or lose their money. Sonny's best friend of thirty-plus years, Dwight, a large 6'3", police officer, provided security, making sure nothing went wrong inside of this illegal gambling operation. Dwight was one of the few people Sonny trusted. They were so tight that Summer only referred to him as Uncle Dwight because she was raised with him as if he was a blood member of her family.

At fifty-seven years old, with only an eighth-grade education, Sonny had accumulated a great deal of wealth. And everything that he had earned had come from the hardcore, dangerous streets. In the late 60s and throughout all of the 70s, Sonny was a smooth talking dope dealer and pimp who mastered the street life of which he was a part.

After finally settling down with one of his main ladies, nine months later his only child, a beautiful baby girl he named Summer, was brought into this world. In 1986, Sonny's wife, Lisa, who was sixteen years younger than him, died from breast cancer; leaving Sonny to take care of their only child. Despite being a singer father, Sonny made sure that Summer had the best education that money could buy. And he spoiled her rotten, giving her everything she ever wanted. Summer was his world, his joy. And if anyone did anything to hurt her, they would surely feel his wrath.

"Hi, everybody," Summer said brightly, walking through the door waving her hand. "Hi, Summer," everyone inside answered back.

Seeing her Uncle Dwight, Summer gave him a pleasant, warm hug and a kiss on the cheek. Walking up to her smiling father, Summer gave him a soft kiss on the lips.

"Hey, Daddy, do you have a minute? I need to talk to you in the back," Summer said. "What is it?" Sonny asked, following his daughter into the back room. "Daddy, I wanted to let you know all of your bills are paid, and I collected the rent money from all of your tenants. I also took care of your car insurance, and I just left your bar and everything was okay. Anything else you need, Daddy?" Summer said pleasantly.

"Yeah, the name of the young man that took you out last night," Sonny demanded. "His name is Prince, Daddy." "Prince! What's his real name?" Sonny said.

"That is his real name. It's Prince Love."

"Malcolm hasn't been in prison for two days, and you're already going out with somebody else," her father snapped.

"Daddy, you know that Malcolm and I broke up. So please, don't start with that again."

"Do you remember what I told you about a man when he goes to prison?" he asked. "Yes, Daddy, how can I forget? Never turn your back on a man who has been sent off to prison because sometimes it can come back to haunt you." "That's right. Your mother waited three years for me, and when I got out I married her, and we had you."
"I know, Daddy, I know. You tell me all the time."

"So what does this Prince fellow do?" her father asked, staring into her eyes. "He works for a real estate company that buys and sells property all around the country," she said proudly. "Well, when do you plan to bring him by so I can meet me?" he continued. "Soon, Daddy. He's out of town right now, but he'll be back tomorrow. So I'll try to set something up then," she promised.

"How long have you known this guy, Summer?"
"Daddy, please."
"Don't Daddy please me. How long?"
"I met him yesterday at the hair salon."
"Yeah, you make sure I meet this guy, you hear me?"
"Yes, Daddy, I will. Bye, Daddy. I just wanted to let you know that everything was taken care of. Latoya is outside in the car waiting. I'll call you later," Summer said, kissing him on his cheek and rushing off.

Washington, D.C.
Later That Night
Sitting inside a rented black Ford Taurus, Prince watched as two white men sat at a table in the back of the

Anna Maria Restaurant on Connecticut Avenue. Moments later, the men exited the crowded restaurant together and walked over to a parked car that was just a few feet away from Prince. After screwing on the silencer to his 9mm handgun, Prince got out of his car and quickly approached them as they stood around talking.

"Excuse me," Prince said. When both men turned around to see who was there, Prince pointed his weapon, then emptied the clip into the heads and bodies of the men. Watching as their lifeless bodies fell to the ground, Prince took out a small digital camera. He took a picture of the two mangled bodies as they lay beside each other in a merging pool of blood. Casually, Prince walked away and got back into his rental car and drove off.

What Summer or no one else had known was that Prince was a hired hit man for the Philadelphia Russian mob. After five years on the job, Prince had killed over fifteen of their enemies.

As Prince drove down the dark D.C. Street, the thought of the horrid deed he had just completed entered his confused mind. Many times, Prince had thought about quitting his dangerous occupation and settling down to have a family. But the twenty-five grand he received for every successful hit was just too good to walk away from. Still, the money wasn't enough to clear his conscious. At night, Prince would be reminded of his sins as his subconscious flooded him with nightmares that left his body dripping in sweat.

After parking his car, Prince went inside of his Holiday Inn suite and took a hot, steam-filled shower to ease his mind. He turned on the news and watched as the animated anchorman reported that two men were found slain inside a parking lot. Prince took a long deep breath, and slowly sipped on a cold glass of water before reaching for the telephone.

CHAPTER 3

Summer

After taking Latoya to the local YMCA to pick up her son, Nolan, from basketball practice, I hurried home so I wouldn't miss Prince's call. Laying on top of my queen size bed, in a white t-shirt and pink Victoria Secrets panties, I talked to Keisha until she ended the call when her man came home. As soon as I heard the phone ring, I grabbed it from the nightstand beside my bed.

"Hello," I answered in my sexiest tone.

"This is a call from a state correctional facility. To accept this call, please press the number five." I reluctantly pressed the requested button on my telephone.

"Yo, what's up, Summer?" Malcolm said sharply into the phone.

"Nothing. How are you doing in there?" I asked.

"I'm okay. I'll be fine. A lot of my homeboys are here. But what you been up to?"

"Nothing much, just running the shop and making sure my father's businesses are right. Boo asked about you. He said that he was going to write you."

"When you see him, tell 'em I said what's up."

"Okay, more than likely he'll be at my father's shop tomorrow, so I'll tell him then."

"What's wrong? Why do you sound like that?"

"Like what?"

"Like you ain't happy to hear my voice. Were you expecting someone else to call you or something?"

"No, I'm just a little tired from working all day at the shop."

"Too tired to hear from me, I see."

"No, it's not like that, Malcolm, and you know it ain't."

"Then why don't you sound happy to hear from me?"

"Because I'm upset with you for being in there. I told you over and over again about the streets and your so-called homeboys. Where are they now? The only person who showed up at your sentencing was your cousin Boo and me."

"Fuck them niggas. I ain't sweating them at all."

"Well, I just want you to know who your true friends are, Malcolm. Those guys that you were hanging with all day and night couldn't even show up at your sentencing to show support. The same guys you always put before me and our relationship."

"Come on, please don't start with that again, Summer."

"Malcolm, I told you that no matter what, I would be here for you. I told you that I won't leave you while you're down, and I meant every word I said. But you know that it's been over between us for a while, and we haven't had sex in months. What we had I could never forget. How could I when you were my first and the only man I've ever been with?"

"So what are you saying, Summer?"

"I just don't want you to be in there worrying yourself about me out here. You got some time to do, and I really hope that you get yourself straight before you come home."

"So will you wait for me?"

"Wait for you? I can't promise you that, Malcolm, and you shouldn't ask me that either. All I can be is a good friend. Something that you will need while you're doing these three years."

"Okay, I can respect that. I'll call you tomorrow. I have to get ready to go. I love you, Summer."

"I love you too, Malcolm."

"Bye," Malcolm said, hanging up the telephone before I could say goodbye.

As the flow of tears began running down my face, I couldn't help but think about Malcolm being away in prison. He had been the only man I had ever loved besides my father. Though I loved him with all of my heart and soul, we were just two different people, with hardly anything in common. I was a young business owner, and he was a young street hustler. I wanted to one day get married and have children while he wanted the new Bentley sitting on 22s. As much as I loved Malcolm, I knew we wouldn't last. But even with the two of us being so totally opposite, I still had given my best to make our diminishing relationship work.

Laying back on my bed, wiping the tears from my watery eyes, the telephone rang again.

"Hello," I said, answering the phone and trying to dry my eyes. Hearing Prince's voice changed my mood and right now it was exactly what I needed. "How are you doing, beautiful? It's me, Prince," his smooth voice said. "I thought you forgot about me," I joked. "Now how could I ever do something stupid like that? I don't think any man could forget someone as beautiful as you, Summer," he said, instantly making me blush.

"Do you always know the perfect words to say?" I questioned. "For the perfect woman, I do," he said without hesitation. "See what I mean?"

"I can't help it. You make me very comfortable, so it's easy to say what I'm feeling to you. I don't know what it is about you, Summer, but you've got me caught up with you, and I need to know more about you and spend more time with you."

"How do I know that you're not just telling me this for your own personal gain?" I asked, leery of his words. "First, I'm not the one to play games, and to be honest, Summer; only time will tell. The moment I saw you, I was blown away. And it wasn't just your beauty; it was your whole presence that made me park my car and follow you into your salon. I enjoyed your company on our date, and I hope that we will get to know each other a whole lot better," Prince said.

"To be honest with you, Prince, I feel something for you as well. And I can't keep you off of my mind. I can't explain it, but it's a feeling that I've never experienced before. I feel like a little girl telling you this but..."
"But what? Go ahead, say it," he said, interrupting me.
"I honestly didn't want our date to end. I hated to see you leave me that night and wanted to figure out a way to say stay with me without sounding desperate."

"Well, maybe next time it won't have to end," he said.
"Yeah, but I kind of want to take things slow. My mind is playing tricks on me, and I don't want to make any more mistakes in my life," I said, probably confusing him and myself. "Life is about making mistakes. That's how we learn to get it right for the next time. You can't appreciate heaven if you've never been through hell."

"Prince, tell me what it is that you want?"
"Happiness. With a capital H."

"Is that all? There's more to life than just happiness."

"Summer, that's all that matters in life. Because once a person finds their true happiness, nothing else really matters."

"Can you explain this happiness?"

"Trust, honesty, faithfulness, commitment, patience, and love all wrapped up in one. Hello. Hello," Prince said into the phone making sure I was still on the line.

"I'm here. I was just lost for a second," I said, shaking my head. "Where did you come from? Who sent you?" I asked.

"I think I should be asking you that question. But I truly believe that when our eyes met, our souls called each other."

"So, let's say you're right. Then what?"

"Then words won't need to be said because we both finally will have our happiness."

For the next few hours, the two of us talked on the phone. I knew I hadn't known this man a week, but I felt a connection to Prince that made me feel as if I had known him for years. The deepness of his conversation was such a comfort and nothing like when I talked with Malcolm. Then when he spoke to me about his physical attraction to me and the ways he would touch, kiss, lick, and suck parts of my body; our conversation elevated to another level. Everything Prince said seemed to have penetrated delicate senses inside my body. And tonight, I had realized things about myself that I had never observed before. There were experiences that I wanted to experience, and a boy couldn't fulfill my requests. This man made me a believer with just his words that he could meet my desires and satisfy my needs.

After finally hanging up with Prince, my pink panties were now soaking wet from the excitement of wanting what was not in the same room as me. In all of my twenty-three years, this was the first time that I had ever cum outside the presence of a man. And even though I had just met Prince and didn't know what street he was raised up on, what was his favorite movie, or where his birthmark was, I wanted to experience making love to him. Maybe I was just caught up in the mysteriousness of him. Maybe I needed a reality check, but either way, I wanted to feel his hands all over me. I wanted to kiss his full lips and see what his body looked like in the nude.

After taking a quick shower, I got back into bed, grabbed my extra pillow and placed it in between my legs. Happily, I closed my eyes and fell asleep.

Early The Next Morning

Inside Sonny's packed barbershop, Sonny, Dwight, and a few friends sat around talking. Leroy, the neighborhood thief, walked into the barbershop holding a brand new microwave oven in his hands and set it down on the floor.

"Sonny, what's up? It's yours for twenty bucks!" Leroy said. "Dwight, lock his ass up!" Sonny joked as everyone began to laugh. "Nigga, you better get that stolen shit out of my barbershop! I told you about that shit," he continued. "Aw, come on, Sonny. Help a nigga out," Leroy said, picking up the black microwave from of the floor.

"I already helped your ass out. Hell, I gave your woman a job at the bar. Why haven't you found a job yet,

Leroy?" Sonny asked. "Man, it's hard out here! Nigga can't get nowhere with an E.G.E.!" Leroy said. "What the hell is an E.G.E., Leroy?" Dwight asked. "Eleventh-grade education," Leroy said, as everyone burst out laughing again.

"Sonny, you gotta minute, man? Please, one minute?" Leroy said, seriously. "What's up, Leroy?" Sonny said, putting his arms around his young friend and walking to the back office in the barbershop.
"Sonny, you know I ain't got nothing but love for you, right," Leroy said. "How much do you need, Leroy?" Sonny asked, cutting him off in mid-speech.

"I need a hundred, Sonny!"
"One-hundred! For what, Leroy?"
"Sonny, I appreciate you giving Wanda the job at the bar, but times is still hard, man. The kids are kicking our ass, man. And I can't keep a job to save my ass. And you know, I be trying."

"You didn't answer the question, Leroy. What do you need a hundred dollars for?" Sonny asked again.
"Next week is Wanda's birthday, and I just wanted to do something for her to let her know that I really appreciate all she does. And to say thanks for putting up with all of my shit. You know what I'm saying? I promise I'll pay you back, Sonny," Leroy said seriously.

"I don't know how I always let you get away with this," Sonny said, going into his pocket and taking out the thick roll of hundred dollar bills. "Here, Leroy," Sonny said, passing him a brand new big face hundred. "Matter of fact, here's another," Sonny said, passing him another hundred dollar bill.

"What's this for?" Leroy said, as his smile grew as wide as his thin body. "That's for next week when you tell me it's your momma's birthday," Sonny said as he grinned. "Thanks, Sonny! I love you, man," Leroy said, getting mushy. "Leroy, just remember youngster, 'Tough times don't last; real Niggaz do,'" Sonny assured. "I'll remember that," Leroy said, walking away with his huge smile leading the way.

"Hey, ain't you forgetting something?" Sonny said. "Oh, my bad, Sonny," Leroy said, putting the microwave back down on the floor before walking out of the door.

That Afternoon
Prince

After returning to Philly from Washington, D.C., I drove up to Bustleton Avenue in Northeast Philadelphia to meet with the Petrov brothers. Victor and Alexander Petrov were the two owners of the Petrov Real Estate Company. This bogus company was no more than a front for the illegal activities of the Russian mob. Victor Petrov was forty-seven years old and the older of the two. He was 6'3", had pale skin, short, dark brown hair, and weighed around 250 lbs. His brother, Alexander, was three years younger and a little shorter, standing at 5'10" and seventy pounds lighter than Victor.

Both of these men were extremely dangerous and ruthless individuals. Control, greed, and money were their only concerns, and with their ambitions at the forefront, they always left a trail of death behind.

Eight years ago I met Victor while in federal prison. I was serving time for a drug possession case, and he was there for money laundering and credit card fraud. The two of us were cellmates, and we had established a solid bond with one other. With Victor's help, I was able to hire a new lawyer, and my case was overturned. Eventually, my lawyer got the case expunged from my records. Before I left prison, I told Victor I'd never forget what he had done for me and if he ever needed me for anything I would be there for him.

Three years later, when Victor was finally released from federal prison, I received a phone call that changed my life forever. One week after that call, I had shot and killed the man responsible for setting Victor up and sending him away to prison. After that unforgettable and blood filled day, I thought I had cleared my debt with Victor. However, one hit, led to a conversation, that led to an envelope that led to me being called to do more hits.

Initially, I considered Victor a very close friend and somewhat of a brother. But as time progressed I often felt like I was being used and taken advantage of. It was because of me that Victor's hands stayed squeaky clean, and his enemies dropped like flies. I played an intricate role for the ruthless Petrov organization, a role where the color of my skin was certainly a bonus for the brothers. Because I was a black man, their enemies never expected me to become their Grim Reaper. Inside of the Russian mob they dealt with their kind, and when it was time to clean up any dirt, that dirt was eliminated by their own. I had become Victor's secret weapon. The job paid well, and I had managed to stay under the radar. But still, every time I took a man's life a part of me died as well. Now killing had become a part of my life, and I feared this unforgivable crime would soon lead to my demise.

"Here you go, Victor," I said, handing him a small white envelope with a picture inside. After taking the picture from the envelope, a grin of satisfaction appeared on Victor's hard pale face. Sitting comfortably in his leather office chair, he began pulling on his long dark brown goatee. Alexander stood behind the desk, also looking at the picture while Victor held it in his left hand. After the two brothers had exchanged some words in their native tongue, Victor stood up and approached me.

"Prince, my good friend, once again you have come through for me," Victor said, patting me on my back. "I knew that I could count on you, my good friend.
"Who were they, Victor?" I asked, already knowing what his answer was going to be. "Prince, how many times must I tell you that you don't need to know any of these people? They are scum, and each of them deserves to die. The less you know, my friend, the better," Victor said, opening up a cabinet drawer.

Every time I asked Victor this question, I would always receive the same answer. "The less I know, the better." For five years I had felt like Victor and his brother Alexander had been hiding something from me. Though they would both deny it, I could tell that a lot more was going on than I had known.

"Here you go, Prince," Victor said, tossing me a large stack of new hundred dollar bills. "It's your money. Thank you once again, my good friend."
"Victor, can I speak to you alone for a minute?"

"Sure Prince. Leave us, Alexander. Let us talk," Victor said, watching his brother walk out of his office, slamming the door behind him.

"What is it, Prince?" Victor said, sitting back down at his desk. "Victor, I have been thinking a lot lately, and I think it's best that you find someone else. I can't keep doing what I do," I confessed. "Prince, must we go through this again? What's the problem, my friend? Is it more money you need? Please, let's talk," he said, trying to see if he needed to increase my payment to keep me on board.

"It's not about money, Victor. It's about me and how I feel afterward," I said, as the faces of those I had killed flashed before my eyes. "Prince, you tell me this every time. Every time you want to quit. Did I quit on you in prison, my friend? Did I leave you like everyone else did you? Like your friends and your family? Or did I listen to you about all the problems you had and decided to help you out, my friend? Victor never turned his back on you, did I," he said, patting himself on the chest.

"No, Victor, you never turned your back," I said, feeling guilty once again about bringing up quitting. "Then why do you always try to turn your back on me? Tell me why?" he questioned. "Victor, you know that's not it at all. I would never do that. I'm just tired."

"Tired of what, Prince, making money?" he laughed. "No, I'm tired of killing people to make money! And I don't even know who it is that I kill or for what reason. All you tell me is that the people I kill are your enemies. That's all you've been telling me for five long years. And your enemy list is longer than a thousand kids' Christmas wish lists."

"You make me laugh, Prince. But, I told you, my friend that they are not good people and all of them deserve to die. Now please, don't ask me about that anymore. Is there something else that you want to tell me, Prince? I feel you want to say much more."

"Yes, I actually did. I met someone the other day. Someone special."

"A woman?" Victor asked, seeing my expression change.

"Yes, a beautiful woman. Her name is Summer."

"So you must really like this woman, huh?"

"She's wonderful. I think I can honestly fall in love with her."

"Prince, you love too easily. You don't know this woman. How can you say words like that about a woman that you just met? Your mouth says foolish words."

"She's different, Victor. She's not like any other woman that I have ever met before. I never felt so strongly about anyone in all my life. Talking to her or being with her makes me feel so complete."

"Is this why you ask me to quit once again, for this woman you met?"

"Yes, she is one of the reasons why I want to quit this life. I have lots of money because of you, Victor, and I will always be grateful. But I want to leave this lifestyle and move on while I still can. I want to start a family and have children one day."

"With this woman, Summer?"

"Yes, I would love that! She's the type of woman I've always wanted to be with."

"Okay, Prince, I see in your eyes that this woman has already grabbed a piece of your heart. But before I can let you move on my friend, I will need you to take care of three more small problems for me."

"Just three?" I said surprised at the small numeric request.
"Just three more and that will be it. After that, you owe me no more favors. And you can be with this woman who has stolen your heart away."
"When do you need it done?"
"I will let you know when I'll need you again. Like always, Alexander will get you a picture of each of them and supply you with everything else you'll need. So after you take care of them, you can go, Prince. You can go, and I will hold nothing against you, my friend, for your decision to quit."

Walking over to his cluttered wooden desk, I happily shook Victor's large hands. Finally, I would be finished with this painful life, I thought to myself. And now maybe my nightmares would come to an end.

After leaving Victor's office, I got into my car and let out a sigh of relief. Though I knew it was wrong, I was looking forward to taking care of these last three targets for Victor. I just wanted it finished so finally I could move on with my life.

Driving away, the thought of Summer entered my cluttered mind. She was able to calm the storms that brew inside my head. I still didn't know what it was about this young woman that had me yearning her, but I had to find out. I once read that there are no right or logical answers for love. We can fight it, and we can run away from it. But love will continue to pull us in and keep us in its tight clutches. I had always been the one who fought, fearing it would take control of my heart. For thirty-three years, I had never allowed anyone to get close enough to penetrate my shield of emotions. I had been in control of whom, when and how I wanted to love. All of that changed as I watched Summer walk across the street that day. I know it's not logical, and many will think I'm crazy for feeling this way about a woman I barely know. But all I can do now is follow my heart and hope that love won't disappoint me.

CHAPTER 4
June 1st
Two Weeks Later

Summer

Prince and I had grown closer with each passing day. The time we spent together was enjoyable and truthfully unforgettable. Though we still hadn't made love, I wanted to feel him deep inside of me more than I had ever desired the touch of a man. But, Prince showed no signs of wanting me in a sexual manner. Yes, he would kiss me so intensely I'd feel as if I was floating high above the clouds, but that was it. And I knew he could tell I wanted him because I couldn't keep my hands off of him, but still, he showed extreme self-control. When he would drop me off at home, he'd always make sure I was safe and then he'd give me a soft kiss goodbye; leaving me craving and wanting him more as I watched him drive away.

I had only been over to his apartment once. And even as we sat down, all cuddled up on his living room couch watching a movie; he still showed no interest in rushing me into his bedroom and giving me what had been on the top of my wish list; the business!

After talking to my girlfriends about what was happening, well really about what wasn't happening, Keisha and Latoya gave me their opinions. Keisha said that he had to be gay because he had unrestricted access to my kitten and he hadn't made a move. Latoya said, "Maybe sex ain't his main concern like every other man, and he just wants to take his time."

I honestly didn't know what to think. I felt lost and confused. Ever since I could remember, men always tried their best to impress me, buying lavish and expensive gifts for me for one purpose only. Sex! Sex! Sex! It was the constant topic of sex that dominated most of their meaningless conversations which always turned me off. But Prince was different. He was the total opposite from all of the other men that I had known. Instead of him being the one pressuring me to have sex with him, it was me who could hardly control myself in his presence. I always wanted an extra kiss or longer hug. I found myself wanting this man so much that it was all I could think about at work and home. Now I was at the point where I had to find out what was going on because I was sexually frustrated. And not because I was horny, but I desired to be with this man who had made me vulnerable to him.

One evening after leaving from my father's barbershop, Prince and I went to dinner and a movie. After leaving the movie theater, I asked to go back to his condominium and just chill. At first, he was a little hesitant, but then he agreed, and the two of us drove to his home.

As we walked into his cozy two-bedroom condominium, I took a seat on the soft tan leather sofa. After kicking off my Gucci sandals, I watched as Prince walked his attractive physique to the radio and turned it on. Suddenly the soulful and jazz stimulated voice of Nora Jones began flowing into the living room air. Prince then walked over to the dimmer switch on the smooth eggshell colored wall and dimmed the bright lights. Going into the kitchen, Prince returned moments later with two small wine glasses and a bottle of sky blue Hypnotiq. He sat the glasses and the bottle on the marble coffee table, as he removed his gray suede and leather Cole Hann shoes, taking a seat beside me on the sofa.

We drank and laughed, as we enjoyed the music and each other's company. Looking into Prince's dark brown eyes, I reached and grabbed both his hands.

"Prince," I said, feeling nervous and tipsy at the same time. "Yes, Summer," he said, with this sexy look on his gorgeous brown face, "What is it?" he asked, waiting for an answer. "Do you mind if I stay here with you tonight?" I asked shyly. Looking into my eyes, "No, I wouldn't mind at all," Prince said, showing me a smile that said he was pleased with my request.

After kissing, drinking and lip locking some more, we retreated into the bedroom. Looking around the large, well-decorated room, it was everything that I had imagined and more. The large queen sized bed sat in the middle of the floor, surrounded by two small glass tables each holding a lit scented candle on top. The beige, lush carpet covered the entire floor. The four white walls each had a colorful abstract portrait hanging from them. One portrait was of a black woman holding a small child in her arms with the words *Unconditional Love* written below. Another colorful portrait was of a black mother, father, and child with the word *Family* written below. Another was a black couple embraced in each other's arms with the word *Happiness* below. The last picture left me speechless, and I couldn't help but stare with confusion. The large painting was a young man, who resembled Prince, holding a gun in his hand while a flow of tears ran down his face. The word below it read *Pain*.

Nothing else was inside of this elegant, and expressive bedroom, but two small speakers that lay beside the bed playing the music from the living room's stereo system. No television, no dresser. And if I hadn't seen the large bedroom closet I would have wondered where he kept his clothing.

Although I wanted to comment about the portrait of the crying man holding the gun, I decided to remain quiet as I sat down on the bed next to Prince.

"This room is so beautiful," I said, looking around. "Thank you. I'm glad you like it," he said, reaching over and giving me a kiss. "Do you mind if I get a little more relaxed?" I asked. "No, not at all, beautiful," Prince said, as he began to unbutton his shirt.

I stood up and slowly removed my clothes. I then placed them in a corner and walked over to the bed and laid down in only my black lace thong and bra set. Prince had removed most of his clothes. Everything except his white Polo boxers and then he laid beside me. As he reached for me and grabbed me into his strong arms, our tongues met with the passion of two distant lovers who had finally reconnected with one another. He then kissed my neck, sending running chills throughout my entire body. My eyes were closed as I felt him remove my bra. He continued to kiss my neck.

After tossing my bra to the floor, he then slid down my soaking wet thong from my faintly trembling legs and tossed it into a corner. As I laid still on the bed, I couldn't help but open my eyes to watch his warm tongue as it traveled slowly up and down my naked body. The feeling was like none that I had ever felt before. My eyes closed tightly as his tongue traveled to hidden valleys that had never been discovered before. Prince mastered the art of tongue blissfulness and as his joyful student, I couldn't do anything but be in awe at the impressive techniques he used on me.

After taking off his boxers and throwing them to the floor, he laid next to me in bed. Looking at his well-toned body, I craved the moment when his rock hard, lengthy, and meaty dick would make its first acquaintance with my dripping wet, warm, kitty.

Staring into my eyes, he reached for my hand. "Summer, I have something to ask you," he said before pausing. "Yes Prince?" I said, feeling my heartbeat beginning to pound inside my chest as my curiosity grew.
"Can I love you without making love to you?" he said in a sensuous tone.

Confused I looked at him and said, "I don't understand what you're saying."
"I want you to spend the night with me, but I cannot make love to you like you want me to," he said to me as the seriousness of his expression made me realize he wasn't joking. "Is something wrong, Prince? Tell me what's going on," I sat up and asked.

"Nothing is wrong, and nothing is going on. And no, Summer, I'm not gay," he said sharply. "Then what is it? Why don't you want me like I want you?" I asked now feeling slightly insecure and still puzzled. "I do want you, Summer, but I want us both to be in love before we make love to each other. I want to be everything you ever desired. I want to be the man you've dreamed about, the one you crave for like no other. I want you so much, but for us to be on a level like no other, Summer, we must first establish a love like we've never felt before. Right now, we want each other's body, but once we begin to yearn for each other's soul, then and only then can we make love. I've had enough sex. That doesn't do anything for me. The taste of your pussy and how juicy it is, I already know how much I'm going to enjoy it. I lust you right now, but I need to build with you. The moment when we have love in our hearts for one another, when we connect, then there will be no words that can explain the full magnitude of how deep making love is. I need that. You're more to me than a quick fix. I want more, Summer. Can you give me that?"

Hearing Prince's deep words caused my eyes to water and brought pleasure to my starving soul. He was speaking to a deeper part of me that many men wouldn't have time to locate or penetrate. Here was a man who wanted me to love him unconditionally. A man that I could see myself being fully committed too, deeply in love with, and plan my future with and around him.

After we had embraced in a kiss filled with the promise of a profound connection, we cuddled together. Being wrapped in Prince's arms I felt safe and protected. This is what I had always wanted. A man that could love me unconditionally like my father, but still cherish me as his own. A man who respects me as a woman: one who insists on loving my soul and spirit before loving my flesh. How could I not fall deeply in love with a man like Prince?

Tonight as our nude bodies nestled in each other's arms, I felt at peace and satisfied. And even though there was no lovemaking involved, this was the best exchange of energy I had ever experienced.

June 8th
One Week Later
Inside Sonny's Upstairs Apartment
Summer

Prince had just walked back outside and gotten into his car, leaving my father and me to talk alone.

"What is it, Daddy, that's so important? We have to hurry and catch our plane," I rushed. "Slow down," he said, going into his pants pocket and taking out a white piece of paper. "Daddy, no, you didn't," I said frustrated. "Yes, I did. Now do you want to know what's the deal or not?" "Daddy, I don't believe you. You're still treating me like a little girl. I can't believe you got Dwight to check out Prince," I fumed.

"So do you want to know or not?" he insisted. "It doesn't matter, does it? You're gonna tell me anyway," I said, folding my arms across my chest. "Well, lover boy's record is spotless. He's thirty-three as he said, and his full name is Prince Jeffrey Love. I also checked up on the real estate company where he works, and so far, everything looks good. But I'ma still keep an eye on him."

"Daddy, are you getting jealous?" I asked. "You're damn right I am. I hardly see you anymore. Either you're at work, or you're out with ole lover boy. I guess you found your prince, huh," he said, with an extra hint of jealousy.

"Isn't that what you've always wanted for me? Didn't you tell me when I was a little girl that if a man can't love me like you, then he isn't worth being with at all," I said, throwing his words back into his face.

"I just don't want to see you get hurt. He's older and more mature than what you're used to," my dad said in a caring tone. "Just like you were with my mother," I smiled. "That was different. I practically raised your mother."

"Daddy, please stop stressing over nothing. Prince is a wonderful man, and to be honest; he does remind me a lot of you. He's sincere, honest, and he's very over-protective of his woman. I feel safe around him, just like I feel when I'm around you," I said assuring him. "Do you love him Summer?"

"Daddy, all I can say is that I have real strong feelings for him," I said happily.

"And what about Malcolm?" The sound of his name instantly irritated me. "Meeting Prince, Daddy, made me realize that I never loved Malcolm. Now I know that it was more infatuation and lust than any love. And being with Prince made me realize that," I said assertively.

"I guess my little girl is growing up."

"Daddy, I've been growing up right before your eyes. You just can't accept that I'm a young woman now. Everything I know is because of you. And I would never be with a man who couldn't give me at least half of the love that you've given. Sooner or later you're going to have to let me go a little bit, Daddy. I just need you to be there for me if I ever have to come back running into your arms."

"You know I'll be right here waiting," my dad said with a bright smile. "I know you will, Daddy. Now I'll call you as soon as we get to Jamaica. I love you," I said, giving him a soft kiss on the cheek and then walking away.

"Don't forget to call me as soon as you get there," he reminded me. "I won't, I promise," I said, rushing out of the door and shutting it behind me.

Before I got into Prince's car, I looked up and watched as my father stared down out of the window at us. Waving goodbye, I got into Prince's Mercedes, and we drove off and headed towards the airport. Prince had wanted to get away, so he asked me to join him in Jamaica. Though it was just for the weekend, I needed this short vacation. Keisha and Latoya could manage the shop while I was away, so I was cleared to go.

As Prince drove to the airport, I couldn't help but stare at him the entire time he was driving. The more quality time we spent together, the more I fell in love with Prince. And even though he never actually said that he loved me, I could tell through his actions that he was falling in love with me too.

CHAPTER 5

Summer

Montego Bay, Jamaica, rich in culture and beauty was one of the most magnificent, and calming places on the face of the earth. The lovely beaches were filled with tall palm trees, crystal white sand, and clear blue water. The temperature was in the mid-90s, as the beaming hot sun shined all throughout this small exotic island. All around the island, sounds of reggae music could be heard. The intoxicating music caused many hips to sway and heads to bob along to the delightful sound.

After we had settled into our stunning, luxurious beach house villa, Prince hired a local escort to show us around. As our tour guide drove us around inside of his three-wheeled motorized carriage, we enjoyed all of the wonderful sights the island had to offer; collecting lots of souvenirs along the way.

When we returned to our private love nest, we showered together, washing each other's body under the warm, soothing water. It felt natural being around each other, so much so that we were completely comfortable with seeing each other's naked bodies. Still, every time I looked at Prince's well-toned physique, I couldn't help but want him. His six-foot muscular frame seemed to drive me wild with every glance.

Once we were both dressed, we decided to go out for a pleasant walk along the shore. Hand in hand, we walked along the beach watching as the sun slowly disappeared beyond the calm blue Atlantic Ocean. As the night fell upon us, we found a cozy spot on the beach and settled down.

Hundreds of shining stars began filling the serene sky. After pulling me into his arms, our lips met with an explosion of passion with each kiss. With our lips entwined, I pulled him in closer, wanting this wonderful feeling to continue.

"Prince, I love you," I said, staring intensely into his brown eyes. "I love you, and I've never felt this way about anyone before. Every time we're together, it feels like a dream. All I can think about is you, all day and all night long. I can't even sleep comfortably without hearing your voice before I fall asleep. And I know it hasn't been that long since we've met, but I know what I'm feeling is true love. I can't imagine you not being a part of my life. I want to give you all of me, and I can only hope for the same in return. I love you, Prince," I said, as my tears of truth and complete vulnerability flowed down my face.

"Is that how you truly feel, Summer?" he said, wiping my tears with his hand. "Yes, Prince, I never felt so sure about anyone in my life," I said, as he kissed my lips and then grabbed my hand and led me away.

Entering our romantic beach house, he started to undress me. After laying me across the large round bed, he started taking off all his clothes so he could join me. Closing my eyes, I could feel his warm tongue navigating around my full sensitive breasts. My perky nipples rose quickly as he sucked on each perfectly, sending shockwaves throughout my body. As he slowly began to descend, he paused and then gave my stomach and navel some much-needed attention. He kissed on my stomach and licked my navel. When he licked my stomach, it was as if his tongue was covered in warming gel. My body heated up, and I was flowing like a juicer, as I sank deeper into the bed clasping the bed sheets.

Prince's large, strong hands grabbed and caressed my thighs. As he spread my legs apart, I watched as he lowered his face within inches of my kitty. His eyes locked with mine as he stuck out his long, husky tongue. He entered my water garden and began stroking my walls with this tongue. I moaned softly as my body shuddered with each tongue stroke. My hands squeezed the sheets tighter, and my legs quaked, as he licked and sucked every crevice inside of my kitten.

As Prince continued to taste me, I felt myself cumming over and over, each time more intense than the last. I had cum many times before but at this moment my body had experienced a feeling like never before. I felt weightless as if I had ascended and was lying on a thick, soft, fluffy cloud. It was as if I had smoked the world's most amazing herbal tonic. All was calm as my pussy gushed an ocean stream of exotic nectar from deep within. The stream was full and powerful as it splashed Prince's face. He licked his lips, tasting my goodness, and when he returned his tongue to my clitoris, my entire body convulsed. It was uncontrollable. I had gone from one extreme of calmness into an intense seizure. And I loved it! I finally understood what it was to experience a sexual orgasm. This was my first orgasm, and although I had had sex before, I swear I felt like a virgin. This man put my body under a spell, and I loved all of his black magic. And just when I thought my orgasm had faded, another one quickly approached.

Taking his precious time, Prince continued to eat my soaking wet pussy like a man on a clear mission, and I climaxed countless times.

Forty-five minutes later, he climbed on top of me as I lay back on the large round bed. I had been pleading with him to touch the part of me that craved him most. And I couldn't believe it was finally happening as I felt his large dick fill every part of my wet paradise; deeply penetrating me with each thrust and robust stroke. He maneuvered his way around my pussy as if he had previously seen the plan to its unique design. He placed me into positions that left me asking myself how he could be so great!

As both of my legs rested on his broad shoulders our lips joined in perfect unison. All night long Prince made love to me, and I felt like a virgin. His touch was new, his lips were like no other, and his thick, meaty, strong dick was one of a kind. Tonight I experienced a night of new and I didn't want to know anything besides what this man had put on me.

After hours of intense, sweaty, lovemaking, we came up for some much-needed air. Exhausted, I flopped in his arms with my eyes shut. Moments later, I felt his hands as he turned me face down onto my stomach. He looked at my ass and then with his right hand he slapped my right cheek with impeccable force. As it bounced, my pussy started to drizzle thinking of the perfect punishment it was about to receive.

Prince arched my back and whispered in my ear, "You have the perfect ass," before entering my pussy from behind. Holding onto the wooden bedpost for support, my constant moans of delight began traveling throughout the room once more. As he continued to stroke deeply, slowly and forcefully, in and out of me, we climaxed together. His drained body slumped down beside me as we breathed heavily. Honestly, I could take no more. I felt like my body had been through a bruising twelve round boxing match. But it had been so damn good that if he had mustered up the energy to go another round, I would have been ready, soaking wet, and open to whatever new moves he wanted to try out on me.

Resting back inside of his comforting and strong arms, we kissed one last time. It was obvious we were dog-tired as our eyes struggled to stay open. Within minutes, we had fallen asleep.

The next day, as the morning sun shined brightly through our large window, I was awakened by the familiar smell of breakfast that lingered in the air. Hot buttermilk pancakes with side orders of cheese eggs and turkey sausages sat next to the bed on a large food tray. I slowly breathed in the wonderful smells as I let out a sigh of delight. I noticed Prince, who had been watching me as I slept, sitting in the chair next to the bed.

"I ordered us some breakfast while you were asleep," he said. "Thank you so much," I replied, stretching my arms over my head. "How do you feel this morning?" he asked. "Wonderful," I said, sitting up in the bed, touching myself to make sure this wasn't a dream.

"I got the shower just the way you like it, nice and warm," he said, flashing a seductive grin. "Did you take a shower already?" "No, I've been waiting for you to join me," Prince said, grabbing my hand and leading me into the bathroom.

As the warm water bounced off our bodies, our lips danced passionately. Clutched tightly in Prince's arms, I felt his large dick enter my wet utopia. As I held his neck tightly with my hands, pleasure filled moans flowed out as Prince picked me up and pounded my pussy. Under the soothing warm water, we had another round of hard, intense lovemaking until we climaxed.

The remainder of our trip, we mostly stayed inside of our beach villa making love. For three days and two nights, we enjoyed each other's love and affection. This romantic Jamaican getaway had opened up the door to a new beginning and countless memorable and unforgettable moments.

Monday Afternoon
Philadelphia, PA

Inside the partially filled hair salon, Keisha and Latoya were in the back room talking.

"Do you think they finally did it?" Keisha said, looking in a mirror fixing her eyebrows. "I don't know, but for Summer's sake, I hope they did. God knows that girl is way overdue," Latoya said, as they burst into laughter.

"Well, she'll be back home tonight and I can't wait to hear every little detail," Keisha said. "Girl, you are so damn nosey. You always want to know what's going on with everybody's sex life, but don't never want to talk about yours," Latoya said seriously. "Ha, ha, you wish," Keisha replied.

"Whoever this person is that you've been creeping around with, you better not let Boo find out," Latoya warned. "Don't worry about me. I got this Ms. Goodie Two-

Shoes," Keisha sassed. "So who is it? And why have you been so secretive about it? Who got you leaving the shop for an hour every day? Because you know I'm getting tired of lying to Boo, telling him you're out buying hair supplies. So who is it, Keisha?" Latoya demanded.

"I can't tell you that," Keisha said, looking at her watch. "If I tell you, I have to kill you, and I don't want my little godson upset with me for killing his mom," Keisha said jokingly.

"Don't tell me you have to make another run Keisha," Latoya fussed. "Okay, I won't tell you. Just watch the shop. I'll be back in about an hour," Keisha said, getting ready to leave. "Girl, you're a trip. But you just go ahead. As usual, I'll make sure everything is taken care of," she said. "Thanks, Toya," Keisha said, rushing to the door. "Be back soon," she yelled as she hurried outside to get inside of her Acura. ~~~

Driving in his silver Range Rover with his right-hand man Cheeze beside him, Ronald "Boo" Watson answered his ringing cell phone. Hearing the pre-recorded prison voice message from his cousin, Malcolm, he quickly accepted the collect call.

"Yo, what's good?" Malcolm said into the receiver. "Same ole shit. Money, hoes and fame. Locking these streets down, and keeping the cops from knowing my name," Boo rhymed. "Yo, I got that money you sent me. Thanks, Cuz," Malcolm said. "Cool. Do you need any more?" Boo asked. "That gee will hold me for a while. But I'll let you know when I need some more dough," Malcolm said.

"Okay. Why you sound so depressed?" Boo asked. "Because I am depressed. Thirty-six fuckin' months, man! This shit is stressing me the fuck out," he snapped. "That time will blow by fast. You just have to stay focused and don't get caught up in no bullshit that will jack your time up," Boo said. "Did you see Summer?" I've been calling her house all weekend, and I keep getting her damn answering machine," Malcolm said, changing the subject.

"Yo, I wanted to tell you..." Boo paused. "Tell me what?" Malcolm interrupted. "She's been seeing this guy named Prince. I met him one day when I went by the salon." "When were you gonna tell me. Next year?" Malcolm said. "No. Actually, I was gonna tell you when I came up to visit you this weekend," Boo said. "So what's up? Is it serious?" "Man, I think so. This dude got Summer on cloud nine and a half."

"That bitch ain't shit! A nigga ain't been locked up a month yet and she already out fucking around," Malcolm angrily shouted.

"I thought you two broke up," Boo reminded his cousin. "Fuck that shit! She's still mine. I'm her first. And I'm gonna be her last," Malcolm snapped. "Man, stop tripping and let her ass go. She ain't no good for you while you're in there anyway."

"That bitch played me! She waited for me to come to prison so she could start fucking around," Malcolm said. "Naw, cousin, you're wrong, dawg. Keisha told me that she met that guy after you got booked. He saw her walking into the shop one day and followed her inside," Boo said. "Oh really. What does this dude look like?" Malcolm questioned, as his curiosity got the best of him. "Bul tall, brown skinned, and oh, he's a little older too," Boo shared.

"How old is he? I know Keisha told you," Malcolm said. "Yeah, you know she tells me everything. He's thirty-three." "So she found herself a sugar daddy, huh," Malcolm laughed. "Look, don't sweat it, Malcolm. Maybe it's just a fling. Someone to fill the void while you're away," Boo suggested. "I thought you said this dude got her on cloud nine and a half?" "I did, for right now. But how many times does a relationship start off on cloud nine and then end up on the sidewalk? Look at all of the shit you and Summer been through over the years. How many times did she catch you messing around and she took your ass right back? She still don't even know about your baby daughter in New Jersey. Man, just give her some space. If she's meant to be with you, she'll be back."

"What if she don't come back? Then what?" "Then fuck it! You lost out to a better man. Don't hate the player, hate the game. You know the rules, Malcolm. How many niggaz' women were you fucking while they were in the joint? What comes around goes around. Don't get mad, cousin, just get your mind right and come back stronger. You got me, dawg. Besides, Summer won't shit on you while you're locked up. She'll write and visit. That's more than what most dudes get, so just chill."

"Alright, Boo, I'ma holla at you in a few days," Malcolm frustratingly said. "Take care, Malcolm. I'll see you this weekend," Boo said, as he hung up his phone.

Taking out a Newport cigarette, Boo lit it and took a long drag. Searching through his loose CD collection that was scattered on the back seat, Boo finally found what he was looking for. Putting the CD into the car stereo, the smooth, soulful R&B voice of Usher flowed clearly through the speakers. Sitting back enjoying the ride, Cheeze began bopping his head to the track.

"This is my shit, dawg!" he said, turning up the volume.
"What's up with Malcolm?" Cheeze asked.
"Nigga trippin' over Summer."
"Why, what's up with them? They still together?"
"Naw, man, they stopped messing around. She been got tired of his shit."
"Then why the nigga buggin' out?" Cheeze said, turning the volume back down.

"'Cause she's fuckin' with some new nigga she just met," Malcolm confessed. "Summer," Cheeze said shocked. "I thought Malcolm had her on lockdown," he continued. "Yup, Summer. I told that nigga if he kept fuckin' up, he was gonna lose her. Women like her only come once in a lifetime, but he didn't listen to me. All he kept saying was how he was her first, and she would never forget him. He was right too— she didn't forget him, she just left his ass. Now he's in prison crying 'cause some nigga's fuckin' his girl and he's got thirty-six months to beat his meat."

Picking up his ringing cell phone, Boo answered, "Speak ya piece," he said. "Okay, yeah, no problem. I can be there tomorrow. I'm a little short, but I'll get the rest. A few weeks, shit is still a little slow! Cops everywhere...Yo, don't worry man, I said I'll have the rest soon. Alright, I'll see you tomorrow. Peace," Boo said, ending the call.

"Who was that?" Cheeze asked. "Tonyman! He wants to see me tomorrow," Boo said. "We ain't finished yet," Cheeze reminded Boo. "I know, but he said he needs whatever we got. So fuck it, he's just gonna have to wait for the rest," Boo snapped. "You know how that crazy nigga is, man," Cheeze said. "Fuck that nigga! He ain't nothing but a whole lotta mouth. You think I take them fake threats seriously? He needs me, just as much as I need him."

Turning the volume back up on the radio, Boo started grooving his head to the music. "Business is business. He just has to wait," Boo said, as he drove on.

~~~

"Oh, Daddy! Oh, Daddy! It feels so good, Daddy," Keisha yelled out, as she reached her sexual peak for the second straight time in less than thirty minutes. Breathing hard and heavy, her body collapsed on the large king sized bed. "Damn, that shit felt good!" she said, feeling the orgasm's aftereffects.

"Will you be able to come back later?" Sonny said, getting out of his bed and checking the caller I.D. on his ringing cell phone. I'll try. My boyfriend wants to go out tonight. But I'll just tell him I have to make a run later." "Don't go through all that trouble. I'll just see you tomorrow afternoon like usual," Sonny said. "Okay. And Sonny, that Viagra ain't no joke. You be fucking me like you eighteen." Keisha said, with a lust filled smile.

"Shit, I need something to keep up with your hot young ass," Sonny laughed, putting on his boxers. "And, you just make sure my daughter doesn't find out that you've been getting this good ole dick for the past six months. I'll never hear the end of that shit," he instructed. "I told you, Sonny, nobody knows about us, but you and me," she promised. "Yeah and keep it that way. I don't want to hurt Summer," Sonny said.

"You should just be happy that she brought me over to your spot. Ever since then you've been fucking me better than my own man has," Keisha said, grabbing Sonny's white robe from off the back door hook and going into the bathroom.

"You just make sure she never finds out!" Sonny yelled into the bathroom. "She won't. Stop worrying," Keisha yelled back, as she showered away the strong sexual aroma from her body.

After showering, Keisha got dressed and walked into the living room. Sonny had just hung up his cell phone and sat in his chair.

"When do you have to be back at the shop?" Sonny asked as Keisha walked next to him. Looking at her watch, Keisha said, "Fifteen minutes," with a huge grin on her face. "Well, all I need is five of them," Sonny said, taking his hard dick from out of his boxers. "You horny old man," Keisha said, shaking her head as she got down on her knees.

Grabbing Sonny's rock hard dick with her hands, Keisha placed it into her warm, wet mouth and started sucking all over it. Sonny sat back in his comfortable chair, enjoying the magnificent feeling Keisha delivered. She continued to swallow him up until he burst deep into her warm, succulent mouth.

CHAPTER 6

Prince

On the plane ride back to Philly, Summer and I sat cuddled together watching as the gorgeous island slowly disappeared from our sight. For three lovely days and two memorable nights, we had enjoyed each other's time and space.

"Did you like your mini vacation?" I asked, looking at her perfectly sculpted face. "I loved it! Lord knows that's what I needed," Summer said with a delighted grin. "What do you think of Jamaica?" I asked. "I think it's the most beautiful place on earth. As long as I live, I will never forget the amazing time we shared there. Heck, one day I could even see myself settling down there. I honestly love it that much! The beach, water, sand, everything about that island is so beautiful. And spending my time here with you was just the icing on the cake," she said, smiling as bright as the sun.

"I love it too. That's why I asked you to join me. And maybe next month we can do it all again? So how's my light shining?" I asked my beautiful companion. "As bright as ever knowing I'll always have you," she said, reaching over and kissing me with her soft, tasty lips.

Summer's Hair Salon

"Where have you been for the last thirty-five minutes?" Boo said as he sat in a customer's chair next to his friend Cheeze, watching as Keisha walked through the door. "I had to make a quick run to the hair supply store on 52nd Street," she said. "Well, where's the supplies then?" Boo said, noticing the only thing in Keisha's hands was her cell phone. "They ran out of the conditioner that we use, so I have to go back tomorrow afternoon. Why? What's up with all these questions?" Keisha said, smiling and waving hello to his friend Cheeze. "Boo, what's up? You know I have heads waiting for me," she said, looking over at Latoya.

"Never mind, never mind. Can I just talk to you in the back room for a minute?" Boo said. "Latoya, is anybody in the office?" Keisha asked. "No, it's empty," Latoya quickly replied. "Come on, Boo. I have to hurry up. I have a two o'clock appointment scheduled."

After they had walked into the office, Keisha locked the door behind them.

"What is it, baby?" Keisha said, putting both her hands on Boo's shoulders. "Something came up, and I have to leave town for a few days," he said. "Where do you have to go this time? You promised me you would take me out to dinner and to see a movie. I was looking forward to our date tonight after I got off of work," Keisha disappointingly said, scrunching up her face like a baby as she lied through her teeth.

"I know, but something came up, and I have to leave town," Boo said sternly. "To where?" Keisha said, acting like a spoiled brat. "New York," he said. "New York! How long are you gonna be there?" Keisha fussed. "For just a few days. I got some real important business to handle."

"Damn baby. I really wanted to spend some quality time together," Keisha said sadly. "I'll be back before you know it. And as soon as I get there, I'll call you," Boo said, holding her face in his large hand and kissing her on the lips. "You promise me?" Keisha said, going from a spoiled brat to a sexy kitten like only she could. "I promise," he said. "Do you need me to do anything before you go?" Keisha said, reaching inside of his Sean John sweatpants. "You know I give the best going away presents," Keisha smiled.

Boo remained speechless as he stood and watched as Keisha took control. Pulling down his sweatpants and boxers, Keisha grabbed his solid hard dick and placed it inside her warm, wet mouth. Boo stood, enjoying the wonderful dick suck that Keisha performed. He had no clue that Keisha had just sucked another man's dick less than an hour earlier.

After watching Keisha swallow every drop of cum that he ejected, Boo remained standing, catching his breath from the breathtaking episode. Grabbing some tissue from a small desk, Keisha wiped around Boo's shrinking dick and then she pulled his boxers and sweatpants back up. She grinned knowing she had just given him an award winning performance.

"Make sure you hurry back home, Daddy," Keisha said. "I will. I told you I'll only be gone for a few days," Boo reminded her. "Okay, but don't make me have to come to New York to find you," Keisha smiled, as she unlocked the door and they walked out onto the work floor.

After Boo had given Keisha a wet kiss on her full lips, he and Cheeze left the hair salon and got back into his Range Rover and drove off. Keisha watched them out of the shop window until they disappeared down the street. Walking back over to her chair that was next to Latoya's, Keisha put on her burgundy apron and called for her customer to come to her seat.

"Next time, save that nasty ass mess for when Y'all are home," Latoya said. With a big Kool-Aid smile on her face, all Keisha could say was, "Stop hating!"

Later That Night
Prince

Inside my center city condominium, after just finishing another intense round of lovemaking, Summer and I lay in my bed talking. Relaxing in my arms, Summer looked up at the four portraits that covered my bedroom walls.

"Prince, what's the meaning of those pictures on your walls?" she asked softly. "Each one has its meaning," I said. "Can you tell me what they mean?" she pleaded.

"Sure. They each mean exactly what they say. The one with the woman and small child in her arms is me as a child being held by my mother. Her love for me was unconditional. No one can love you like your mother. And that one with the woman, man and child is what I've always wanted. A family. I never knew my father. He ran out on my mother and me when I was a child. He had another child with a woman, who he also ran out on. So I have a brother, but we don't talk. There is no real connection between us besides the DNA of a nonexistent father.

That one over there, with the two people, embraced in each other's arms, is what I call my *Happiness*. It's two people who are not just madly in love with one another, but they are also soul mates. And once a person finds his or her soul mate, true happiness is right around the corner."

"Am I your soul mate, Prince?" Summer asked, looking into my eyes. I smiled slightly as I leaned over and gave her a soft kiss on the lips because I was not ready to answer her question.

"Can you tell me what that portrait means?" Summer asked, pointing to the last one on the wall. "It represents what it says. Pain! It's a portrait of my deepest fears," I confessed. "What is your deepest fear?" she said now concerned. "To live without being able to experience the first three. Unconditional love, family and happiness." "Why wouldn't you live to see that?" Summer asked confused.

"Because nothing in this world is promised. And everything that I have loved was taken away from me. I lost my mother. I never knew my father. And I have no family. All I have is me. Me, me and me."

"Well, now you have me and I ain't going nowhere, Mr. Love," Summer said, rolling over and climbing her naked body on top of mine.

"Maybe God brought us together so we could give each other all the things in life that we both desire. I know that I love you, and I would never do anything to hurt you, Prince. I honestly believe in my heart that you are my soul mate," she said sincerely.

Summer and I kissed intensely as the feeling of love warmed our bodies. Maybe she was right. And maybe she was the special woman that God had always had for me. At that moment, I prayed that she was the one.

Northeast Philadelphia

The round wooden coffee table was filled with stacks of fresh hundred dollar bills. On the floor, brand new 9mm handguns were packed neatly inside brown cardboard boxes.

Four AK-47 Russian military machine guns stood along the wall. Boxes of ammunition and a few bulletproof vests were also inside the small apartment that Victor and Alexander secretly occupied. From murder to gun smuggling, credit card fraud to extortion, you name it, and Victor and Alexander were a part of it. In 1976, the two young brothers escaped to the United States from a brutal and violent group of mobsters, leaving their entire family to be massacred by a powerful ruler and his treacherous regime.

After watching his mother's and father's execution, along with his two older brothers', Victor swore to himself that one day he would take revenge against his family's murderers. For years, he and Alexander had gathered information on all of the men who played a part in killing his family. Now for five years, he had been using Prince to murder each of these ruthless men, one by one. Whenever one of his enemies would make a trip to the United States, Victor was notified by his close connects in Moscow that they were headed to his current turf. With money, Victor had amassed a lot of power. And with his power, he could personally track down each of these men until there was no one left to kill.

Holding a small picture in his hand, Victor slammed his fist hard on the wooden table, knocking piles of money to the floor. "Ya hachu stobe on umero!" he yelled out, squeezing his fist tightly. "I want him dead!!!" he yelled out, this time in English. "I want him dead!!!"

"Don't worry, Victor, we will get him, brother," Alexander said, comforting his older brother on the sofa.

"He took away our family, Alexander! He killed them all," Victor cried out. "And he will pay for every drop of their blood," Alexander angrily said.

The small picture was of a man who looked to be in his mid-60s to early 70s. His name was Boris Novikov. The man who had ordered the brutal execution of Victor and Alexander's family. The man that Victor had been obsessed with killing for over twenty-five years.

As this hefty man with a heart filled with rage sat back in tears, his younger brother continued to console him. Through all of their struggles, trials and tribulations, all they had in this lonely, cold, cruel world was each other.

New York City

Lying in bed with two beautiful naked young women, Boo reached over and grabbed his cell phone from off the dresser. Shakira and Joy were just two on the long list of NYC women that Boo would call for sex whenever he was in town for business or in this case, pleasure.

"Be quiet y'all. I have to call my girl back in Philly," Boo said. Both girls started kissing one another as Boo talked into his cell phone.

"Hello," Keisha answered. "Where are you? I called you, and the answering machine picked up. So what I got to do, track you down now," Boo said. "I'm out with my sister. We're at Scooters Bar having a few drinks. Is everything okay?" Keisha asked, worried by the tone of his voice. "Yeah. I'm fine. I just wanted to make sure you were okay. I'll be back home Wednesday morning," he said. "Take your time, baby; I'll be here waiting. Just handle your business," she said.

"Okay and don't be out too late. You know how those crazy ass bottom niggaz be acting at Scooters," Boo demanded. "I'll be okay. I'm not paying them niggaz no mind. Besides, they know who my man is," Keisha said proudly. "Yeah, they know better," Boo smiled, filled up with arrogance.

"Why is it so quiet?" Boo asked, becoming suspicious. "Because I'm in the bathroom. When I saw it was you calling I came in here so I could hear you," Keisha said. "Well, I'ma call you in the morning. You be safe. I love you."
"I love you too, baby. See you soon."

After ending the call with his girlfriend, Boo immediately joined the two women who had been patiently waiting for their Philly stud to return.

Inside A Small Apartment In West Philly

"Now where were we?" Keisha said, rolling her naked body back on top of her friend. "You were just about to show me your famous horseback riding skills," the man said smiling. "Oh, that's right," Keisha said, sliding his stiff dick back into her wet creamy pussy.

As he lay back enjoying the wetness of Keisha's paradise, she began to ride him just the way he liked it; nice and slow. Every time Boo went away on business, Keisha would take care of some business of her own. She and her secret lover would get together for bouts of lustful sex. Being with her lover wasn't about money or materialistic items that he could afford to buy her. It was strictly for sex. Something they both enjoyed sharing with each other.

A Few Hours Later
1:35 A.M.
Summer

Walking from the bathroom, I noticed Prince staring hard at the "Pain" portrait on the wall. Sneaking up behind him as he stared in a deep gaze, I gently grabbed him. Caught off guard, he quickly did some type of martial arts move and reversed my grip, and now he had me in his arms.

"That's not fair, Prince! Show me how you did that," I said. After showing me the move a few times, I had it down pat. "I see you're full of surprises," I said, again trying the martial arts move on him. "Not that many, just a few," he said, as he easily broke out of my hold and carried me back to the bed.

New York City

Covered in pouring sweat, Boo had Shakira bent over the bed fucking her in the ass. On the opposite side of the bed, Joy held down both of Shakira's hands. "Ohh, Papi, oh, Papa, Fuck me! Fuck me! Yes! Yes!!!" Shakira yelled out. Pulling his dick out and cumming all over her back, Shakira's sweaty body slumped deep into the bed. "It's your turn, Joy," Boo said, as the females switched positions.

As Boo now fucked Joy in her anus, her loud scream-filled moans packed the foggy hotel room. Hearing a loud and sudden knock on the door, Boo was forced to stop and investigate.

"Who is it?" Boo said, standing naked behind the door. "The hotel manager," a male's voice said. "Open up!"

Boo quickly opened the door, but just enough for his head to stick out.

"What's up?" Boo said, as the sweat fell from his head and he tried to calm his heavy breathing. "Sir, I've been getting numerous complaints all night long from the other guests on this floor. Can you and your friend or friends or whatever please keep down the noise? If not, I'm sorry, but I'll have to ask you and your company to leave," the snooping short white man said.

"Yeah, alright, we'll keep it down," Boo smirked, knowing that he was now the talk of the entire third floor. "Please, sir, I don't want to have to come back up here," the man said, as he began to walk away. "Alright, Shorty, I said we'll keep it down," Boo said, slamming the door.

Returning to the bed, both girls started laughing about the hotel manager's visit.

"I guess we're gonna have to keep it down, huh?" Shakira said, grabbing a pillow as Joy got back into position.

CHAPTER 7

Tuesday Morning
Summer

"So what else happened?" Keisha curiously asked, craving more of the sex-filled conversation that Summer had been sharing with her and Latoya. "That was it. I told Y'all everything," Summer smiled, watching as her best friends yearned to know more about her three-day sex packed adventures with Prince.

"So clearly he ain't gay?" Keisha said. "Not a gay bone in his body. And I can vouch for that," I said proudly. "I told you, Keisha, that he wasn't gay. You think every man is either a dog or gay. But there's still some good men running around. And Lord knows I can't wait to find me one," Latoya said. "What? You got one. Your new neighbor, Mr. Smith," Keisha said. "No. We're just friends, that's all," Latoya blushingly said. "Yeah, okay," Keisha said, smiling.

"Anyway, girls, my trip to Jamaica was wonderful! So good that we are going back next month for another romantic getaway," Summer said. "You lucky Bitch! I can't even get Boo to take me to a Jamaican restaurant," Keisha said, as the three of them laughed hysterically at the joke.

"So was I right, Summer?" Keisha asked. "Right about what?" I asked, wondering what she was talking about. "You know, the Big-O," she said. "Oh," I said, as my smile grew so big it now covered my face. "Yes! You were right! My whole body trembled. I couldn't control my legs at all. I felt like I was having an out-of-body experience. At one point I swear I felt like I was about to faint."

"Well, well, well," Latoya said, shaking her head as she took it all in. "Next time you talk to Malcolm, you should cuss his five-minute ass out for wasting all of those precious years," Keisha said. "Leave me alone, Keisha," I said, playfully pushing her shoulder. "Some people just need more practice than others," I continued. "No, some people just need a bigger dick and a course on pre-ejaculation skills," Keisha said.

Walking out from the office in laughter, the three of us returned to work. As we worked, we couldn't help but erupt into mini laugh sessions. Our customers had no idea what was so damn funny. I wondered if Malcolm's ears were now burning, knowing that someone was talking so badly about his sexual performance. But, I let that thought go and got back to work.

As usual, Keisha had to make a run during lunchtime. Latoya and I talked and laughed about her obvious errand until she returned. Once back, Keisha sat down in her chair next to Latoya and me. Keisha didn't have to tell us what she had just finished doing; it was obvious.

Ever since junior high school, Keisha had been a sex-crazed, energetic teenager. The only thing she enjoyed more than sex was shopping. In high school, there was a rumor going around that Keisha was sleeping with Mr. Jacobs, our math teacher. I guess our peers were too young to fill the sexual void she had. And the only solid proof we had that she slept with Mr. Jacobs came when she passed his Algebra III class with all A's. Keisha wasn't the type of student to get good grades in math, so it was clear she had given up the goods to get the A's.

Keisha had always had a thing for older, more established men. That's why she was with Boo. He was four years older, extremely handsome, and he also had it going on in the bedroom and in his pockets. Boo started out as a petty young hustler on the streets of North Philly, and eventually became the leader of a small crew of thugs. In less than four years Boo went from being fronted 4½ ounces to work off for someone else, to now buying multiple kilos of cocaine to supply his growing street enterprise. And Keisha was thoroughly impressed with each and everything Boo had going on.

She loved when Boo would surprise her with extravagant gifts, such as cars, jewelry, and expensive designer clothes. And as long as Keisha continued to fuck Boo the way he desired and played her part as wifey; he gave her the world on a silver platter. And she accepted everything he gave and often requested more.

Suddenly, a short, dark-skinned man in a thin beige jumpsuit walked into the salon and approached the three of us. Inside of his hands, he held a large white box with a red bow around it.

"Excuse me, is there a Ms. Summer Jones that works here?" he politely asked. "Yes, that's me," I said, smiling. "This is for you," he said, handing the large white box to me. "Can you please sign for it?"

"What is it? Who is it from?" were some of the immediate questions I had as I struggled to hold the large box in my hands. "It's from... oh, here it is, Mr. Prince Love," he said, looking at a small piece of paper. How could I not smile as I signed for the delivery and watched the man hurry out the door?

"Open it up! Hurry up!" Keisha and Latoya said as I sat down between them with the box on my lap. "Hold on," I said, untying the red bow. Opening the box, the three of our eyes were locked on the package as we eagerly looked inside.

"Oh my, she is so cute," Latoya said, smiling from head to toe. "Yes, she is," Keisha said, hugging me as I stood up with tears falling from my eyes. I was totally surprised.

Inside the large white box was the cutest all white Samoyed puppy that I had ever seen. Cuddled up inside the corner of the box, she looked up at me with her pretty blue eyes. I was speechless and in total shock. All I could do was cry. Seeing the small white envelope taped to the inside of the box, I grabbed it and opened it. Inside the envelope was an original handwritten poem from Prince. The name of the poem was *Soulmates*. As the flow of tears continued to drop down my face, I began reading the poem to myself.

I surrendered my love to you because I knew you would not take it and run away.
This burning feeling that's inside of me has now turned to flames. Flames of joy and passion.
Love crept up on me and caught me by surprise. Off guard. Out there.
Was it heaven that sent you cruising into my empty world? Or were you sent straight from God himself with the message of love written across your heart?
I never understood love until you appeared holding a pamphlet filled with its rules and regulations.

Now you're my heaven on earth. Bringing me an abundance of wonderful emotions that I never knew could exist.
You now have a large piece of my soul all to yourself. And I trust you exclusively to take care of it.
Your Soul Mate, till this world is no more, and the next one awaits us both.
Love, Prince.

After allowing Keisha and Latoya to read the tear-jerking poem that Prince had written for me, they too were emotional. I was so touched by his words and the beautiful puppy that I took the rest of the day off.

Driving home with my adorable little Samoyed puppy sitting beside me in the passenger seat, I just couldn't stop crying.

"Hey, cutie," I said, gently rubbing on her little forehead. As she licked my hand, I thought about what I would call her. Then it hit me. "Love. That's what I'll call you, cutie. Your name will be Love," I said, looking into her gorgeous baby blue eyes. Ever since I was small, I had always wanted a dog, but my father would never let me have one. He would always say that all a dog does is eat, sleep and shit. Now I finally had my own little eating, sleeping, and shitty puppy that I named Love. And she was truly the cutest puppy that I had ever laid eyes on.

Pulling into my townhouse driveway, I parked my car and then reached over and grabbed Love from off the seat. As I walked up to my front door, I burst out laughing. I thought about what Keisha had said earlier. And yeah, maybe the next time I talked to Malcolm on the phone, I should cuss his no-good, five-minute, little dick ass out for wasting so much of my time.

Manhattan, New York

The calm New York sky was quickly darkening as the large crowds of people hurried to get where they were going. Bright yellow New York City cabs drove wildly up and down the cluttered streets. Food vendors cramped the crowded sidewalks selling everything from hot dogs to steak combos. Music from all genres filled the air. New York was like no other place on earth. The city that never sleeps is what they call it. Fast women fast cars and fast money. This city had everything a young hustler from Philly desired.

Boo sat inside his Range Rover thinking. Seeing Tonyman pull up in his black Mercedes Benz CL600, Boo stepped out of his Range Rover holding a white plastic bag in his hand and got inside of Tonyman's car.

"What's up, Boo?" Tonyman said, as he slowly pulled off and drove down the street. "Same ole, same ole. Here's ya money," Boo said, passing Tonyman the bag. "How much is that?" Tonyman said looking inside of the bag as it lay in his lap. "Eighty thousand. I'll have the rest soon," Boo said. "When the fuck is soon, Boo? Something big is coming through. You know it's a drought here out on these streets. I need the rest of my fuckin' money." Tonyman shouted.

"Tone, I said I'll have it for you soon. Stop trippin', man. It's me, Nigga. Did I ever fuck up your money before? Now, I can't make the shit grow on trees, dawg," Boo said. "Well, you better start planting some seeds in a hurry, 'cause I'ma need my other two-twenty," he said seriously. "Yo, as soon as I knock the rest of this shit off, I'll call you and drive back up."

"Make it fast! I got niggaz on my ass, so I'ma stay on yours," Tonyman said. "Don't make me have to do nothing stupid, Boo. I like you, Nigga, but business is business. I'll call you soon," Tonyman said, pulling over to the side of the road.

After getting out of the car, Boo watched as Tonyman sped off down the street. Boo walked back to his parked Range Rover that was a few blocks away. Once inside of his SUV, Boo pulled out of his parking space and drove off.

As he headed towards the Lincoln Tunnel to return to Philly, Boo made a sudden U-turn. Dialing a number on his cell phone, he waited for someone to pick up. "Hello," a voice answered. "Yo, I just saw him. I'm on my way back," Boo said, ending the call.

Later That Night

Inside her small apartment, right above the hair salon, Latoya sat at the kitchen table playing a board game with her son, Nolan. Hearing a soft knock at the door, she walked to see who it was. Looking out of her small peephole, Latoya smiled and quickly opened the door.

"Hey, Earl," Latoya said, standing in the doorway. "Hi, Latoya, I just wanted to know if you could let me use your phone again. The phone company will be out tomorrow to hook mine up," he said. "Sure, come in. It's over there," Latoya said with a broad smile, pointing to the telephone that was sitting on top of the living room table.

"Thanks, Latoya, I appreciate it, sweetie," Earl said, walking inside of the apartment. "Hi, Mr. Earl," Nolan said.

"Hey, Lil man, how's that jump shot coming along," he asked. "I did what you showed me and I finally scored a basket," Nolan said proudly. "I told you, you would. Shoot up and let the ball roll off of your fingertips," Earl said, showing Nolan his shooting form.

Two weeks ago, Earl Smith had moved downstairs into the vacant apartment. He was very tall, medium build, chocolate with short dark hair, and he had a small, light-colored birthmark on the right side of his neck. His looks were average, but he had a dynamite personality that made you look at him as if he was the most handsome man in the room.

Earl was a former European professional basketball player who was now working as a gym teacher at the nearby high school. From the first day he and Latoya met, they hit it off; smiling every time they passed each other in the halls coming or going to work. At 6'5", Earl was a giant among dwarfs, and Latoya liked every bit of it. Some nights after Nolan was dead asleep, Earl and Latoya would sit inside her living room and talk for hours. Though they had only met a few weeks ago, already some feelings were starting to form.

Still, Latoya was very cautious about who she allowed around her child. So Earl could only come over to spend time with her once Nolan was in bed asleep. She never thought about bringing any man in the same space as her young son, until Earl moved downstairs.

Celibate for over a year, Latoya was way overdue for some sexual satisfaction. But unlike her best friend, Keisha, she was not running an all-night, 24-hour hit and run deli. Since a failed relationship with Nolan's father, Latoya picked and chose her men very wisely. And so far, Mr. Earl Smith was doing and saying all the right things, while Latoya was hoping and praying that she had finally found the man who could earn her love, joy and affection.

Summer

Laying in my bed with my beautiful Samoyed puppy, I reached for the ringing telephone. "Hello," I answered with a smile, already aware of who was calling.

"Hey, beautiful, it's me, Prince."

"Hey, baby, I was just thinking about you. Did you finish everything you had to do today?"

"Yeah, I had some business to take care of, but everything's fine now. What's up?"

"Thank you so much, Prince, for giving me, Love!"

"Love? Who's Love?"

"My new puppy you bought me! I named her Love."

"Love, I like that. It's original."

"I couldn't believe my eyes when I opened that box today! She looked so cute. I swear I couldn't stop crying when I saw her. Thank you so, so much, baby!"

"I'm glad you like her, Summer. I saw her in the window of a pet store, and I knew you wouldn't be able to resist those pretty little blue eyes."

"She's right here in bed with me now, keeping me company because you're not here."

"Is that a hint? Because I could be there in about a half hour."

"Then what are you waiting for?"

"I'm on my way over now. Don't fall asleep."

"Only if you put me to sleep...I'll see you when you get here."

"Sorry, Love, but Daddy's on his way and three's a crowd," I said, putting Love back inside of her box which for the moment was her temporary home.

~~~

"I enjoy being with you, Latoya," Earl said, sitting on the living room sofa with his arm around her shoulders. "Every day I wake up I look forward to seeing you before I go to work," he continued. "Earl, I think we should take things slow. I told you before that I haven't been with a man in a very long time. And as much as I like you, Earl, I think it's best that we both take our time. I promise you; I'm worth the wait and not only will you appreciate all that I have to offer, but you'll also respect me. I really hope that's not a problem because I honestly enjoy your company," Latoya said, clearly getting her point across.

"First, let me say I do respect you, Latoya. You're a beautiful, independent, single black woman who's raising a future king alone. I'm in no rush, at all. And I know you'll be worth the wait," he said smiling, reassuring her he was in no hurry. "Thank you, Earl, I appreciate that," Latoya said, as she reached over and gave him a quick kiss on the cheek. Even though Latoya meant every word she had spoken, she still felt that every night the two of them sat around talking, her sexual defense shield was slowly beginning to dwindle.

"Tomorrow night, same time, same place?" Earl said, standing in the doorway. "Same time, same place," Latoya said, as she stood on her tiptoes and gave Earl a soft kiss on the lips. "Make sure you tell, Nolan, to keep practicing that jump shot I showed him," he said. "I will," Latoya smiled.

"Bye, beautiful. I'll see you in the morning," Earl said, walking down the hallway. "Bye, Earl," Latoya said, watching him as he walked away.

After closing the door, Latoya rushed into her bedroom and locked the door. Reaching under her pillow, she pulled out a small black vibrator and started playing with her wet pussy. As she climaxed quickly, she couldn't help but wish that it was her handsome, tall, chocolate neighbor making her tap out instead of her toy.

~~~

The lights were dimmed, and the aroma of sweet incenses burned throughout the bedroom. Love watched from her box as Prince had Summer bent over the bed, fucking her from behind. With every stroke, her hard moans filled the scented air. As her long manicured nails dug deeper into the blanket, Summer could feel every single inch of Prince's enormous dick penetrating her gushing walls.

Summer never imagined that the perfect amount of pain could cause so much pleasure. She wanted more of Prince; deeper, harder, stronger, and without hesitation. He was providing her with a sexual healing and a beating at the same time.

"Ahhhhhhh," Summer yelled out as the strong orgasm ran throughout her naked body. Her tired gorgeous physique collapsed onto the bed. However, Prince continued to hold onto her shapely hips until he finally came inside of her. Falling by her side, their two perspiring bodies lay on top of a bed of wetness. Summer could still feel her pussy trembling from the sexual pounding Prince had given it. This was the type of encounter she yearned and welcomed.

Once their late night XXX-rated episode had concluded, Love sat back down in the corner of her box and fell asleep along with her new owners.

CHAPTER 8

Wednesday
Summer

Early the next morning, I awoke to Prince's soft, plentiful lips eating my pussy. After the pleasurable beating my kitten had taken the prior night, this early morning clitoral stimulation had worked wonders. Prince knew precisely what to do to turn me on, and eating my pussy before the sun had risen was numero uno on the list.

After a morning quickie and a steamy shower together, Prince and I needed to leave my house. He had received an important call just as we got out of the shower, so he had to rush out. I was running late, and this was certainly not a trait that I was about to get used to, so I had to get moving also. Prince kissed me on my lips and then he drove off, as I waved goodbye and rushed to get into my car.

Walking into the salon forty-five minutes late, Keisha and Latoya were already at work on their client's heads. Showing up for late work was not my thing, and they both knew it. It was me who always stressed that everyone should arrive to work on time.

"E.M.P.M.?" Keisha said, smiling. "What, girl? What is an E.M.P.M.?" I curiously asked, taking my work apron off the rack and putting it on. Looking over at Latoya's smiling face, I figured she knew what the acronym meant.

"Early morning pussy massage," Keisha said. "I know that look from anywhere." All I could do was laugh and clearly everyone in the salon felt the same way as they joined in with their giggles.

"Girl, you're crazy," I said, feeling super embarrassed. "Don't be ashamed, Summer," shouted Niki, a regular customer who was getting her hair done by Latoya. "I wish one of these mornings I could get me an E.M.P.M. from my lazy ass husband. Hell, after fifteen years of marriage, I can barely get fifteen minutes a week from his ass," Niki said, and everyone laughed.

"Summer, you got a minute?" Keisha said, walking towards the back office. "What's up?" I said, following her into the back. "I need to make a run in about an hour. Can you take care of Cynthia for me?" she asked. "Why, what's up? It's only 9:15 in the morning. You usually take your break in the afternoon," I said. "I have a doctor's appointment at the Medical Clinic at 10:30."

"Keisha, you don't have to lie to me. You know I'm gonna say yeah anyway," I told her. "I'm serious, Summer. I do have an appointment. See," Keisha said, showing me a small white doctor's note with the time and date for her appointment.
"Oh, I just thought you wanted to get away for a quick E.M.P.M.," I laughed. "No, I already had one of those," Keisha said. "What? I thought Boo was in New York," I said. "He is, but my vibrator is in Philly," Keisha said, as we laughed before walking back onto the work floor.

Northeast Philadelphia
Prince

"What's up, Victor? I hurried over here," I said, walking right past Alexander and approaching Victor's cluttered desk. "I have another job for you, Prince," Victor said, passing me a small Polaroid picture. "Where is he?" I asked as I looked at the photo. "He's in Chicago," Alexander interrupted, standing up from the couch.

"The windy city, huh? When do you want me to leave?" I said. "Tonight. Alexander will make sure you have everything you need," Victor said. "Okay, I'm on it," I said. "Alexander, go get everything ready. I have to talk with Prince," Victor said, in his deep Russian accent.

After Alexander walked out of the office and shut the door, I took a seat on the empty sofa. "What's up Victor? What is it that you want to talk about?" Victor crossed his arms and said, "I want to know if you changed your mind, Prince." "No, I told you, Victor, after I take care of these final three men that I was through. And I meant it. My word is my word."

"What if I added ten thousand to each future hit?" Victor asked. "It doesn't matter if you add twenty more, I'm through when these final three are gone," I said solidly. "This woman that you've been spending time with has changed you I see," he said. "Victor, yes I'm in love! Maybe it doesn't mean anything to you, but it means the world to me. I've finally found my happiness, and I won't let anything or anyone take it away from me."

"I admire you, Prince. You are truly a good man. I hope you and this young woman do find happiness, because out of everyone I know you deserve it. And I will not ask you anymore to reconsider. Your meaningful words speak to me in volume. After the last three, my good friend, you go and enjoy your life. And I will always be here for you if you need me."

"Thank you, Victor. I'm glad you understand," I said, looking at the photo once more.

~~~

Keisha had a perplexed look on her face as she drove back to the salon. Her early morning appointment had brought her quite the surprise. On the short ride to the shop, she didn't have enough time to fully comprehend the recent news she had just received. And before she knew it she was within minutes of reaching her job. After a long sigh, she parked her car and went inside the hair salon.

Prince

"Hello," Summer said, answering the telephone.
"Hey, baby, it's me," I said smiling as I heard her sweet voice.
"I was just thinking about you. What time are you coming over tonight?" Summer asked. "That's why I called you, sweetie. I have to go out of town tonight," I said, internally hating myself for the mission I had to complete.

"Aw, baby, I was looking forward to seeing you tonight. Where do you have to go?" she asked, disappointed.
"I have to be in Chicago tonight."
"Chicago! For how long?"
"Just a few days. I'll be back on Saturday."
"You sure? You know I can't go too long without my beef-stick," Summer said seriously.

"You just hold that craving until I get back. I'll take care of it," I said, laughing at how serious she was about getting some. "I love you, Prince. You be safe and call me as soon as you get to your hotel," she demanded. "I will, my love. And I love you too. Talk to you later," I said, as we ended the call.

Summer

"What's wrong with you?" I said, looking at the disorganized look on Keisha's face as she hung up the phone. "Nothing. I'm just a little tired; that's all," Keisha said, sounding nothing like her normal cheerful, playful self. "So what did your doctor say?" I asked, feeling that something was wrong. "He said I was fine. I have to see him again in two weeks," she said. "Then why do you look like something is bothering you?" I meddled. "I'm okay. Like I said, I'm just a little tired. That's all," Keisha said, putting on her apron and walking over to her chair.

I knew Keisha better than anyone, and something was bothering her. As I watched her braid a customer's hair, I could tell something heavy was on her mind. Keisha was the type of woman who wants to know everything about you, but will never fully open up about herself to anyone. And when she does finally get around to telling me and Latoya what's been troubling her, it's weeks later when it doesn't matter anymore. Today something was weighing on her. And from the look on her face, Latoya and I might find out what's up much sooner than later.

After several attempts to break her silence, I stopped trying to get any information out of Keisha for the day because she wasn't budging. I went back to work, closed up shop, and went home disappointed because I knew I couldn't see or touch my man. Later that evening as I watched television with Love, who feel asleep beside me in bed, my telephone rang.

"Hello," I said, answering the ringing telephone. Hearing the scripted prison voice recording from Malcolm, I unintentionally accepted his phone call.

"What's up Summer?" he asked. "Hey, Malcolm. Did you get the money and pictures I sent you?" I said, frustrated with myself for accepting his call. "Yeah, I got it the other day. Thanks. So what's going on with you? When are you gonna come out and visit a nigga?" he said, sounding desperate. "I've been real busy lately, but I'll try to get up there to see you soon," I lied.

"What's soon? A week or two?" he pressed. "I don't know, as soon as I can find some free time. You know, I gotta run my shop and take care of my father's business too." "Summer, you don't have to lie to me! I know about this new friend you got. I hear things," he said. "No one's lying to you. I was gonna tell you about him, Malcolm," I lied again. "When? When Y'all was on Y'all honeymoon?" Malcolm upsettingly said.

"It's not like that! We're just good friends."
"So a good friend just takes you to Jamaica for the weekend, huh?" he snapped. "Who told you that?" I fumed feeling betrayed that someone had told Malcolm my personal business. "It doesn't matter who told me. How the fuck you gonna cross a nigga like that?"

"Malcolm, I didn't cross you, and you know it! You do know it has been over between us! We haven't had sex in months, and that was before you even went off to prison. When you were out here fucking all those bitches, you couldn't find no time for me. So don't act like you care now! Now you're locked up, and you want to put your foot down like you're my damn father! Don't try to change this shit around on me, Malcolm! You know you did me dirty, and I still showed you nothing but love," I shouted at this ungrateful bastard.

"So you couldn't wait? Three years ain't shit to do," he said as if he hadn't heard anything I had said to him. "Things happened, Malcolm. I didn't think I would meet someone. And why should I stop and put my entire life on hold for you? Would you do the same thing for me if the situation was the other way around? Would you wait and be faithful to me?"

Malcolm suddenly was as quiet as a mouse because he knew he couldn't commit to me when he was on the streets, so how could he hold me down if I was the one behind bars.

"Yeah, that's what I thought," I continued, throwing the truth all up in his face. "Look, I'm just saying how do you think I feel? As soon as I get locked up, my girl finds her some new nigga and flies off to Jamaica with him. That's fucked up," he said. "First of all, Malcolm, I'm not your girl anymore. And second, if I choose to let someone take me away, it's my business. So cut that act! We are over, and nothing I do in regards to who I see or screw is any of your concern!"

"Can I just ask you one question?" Malcolm said. "Don't ask me a question if you can't handle the answer," I said. "Do you love this dude?" he said, all the way in his feelings. "Malcolm, please," I said, brushing the question off. "Just answer the question, Summer," he demanded. "Malcolm, please, don't do this," I said, not seeing the point of him knowing how I felt about another man.

"So you love this nigga, huh? Some muthafucker you just met got you all strung out," he snapped. "I didn't say that. You did," I said, without denying that I did love my Prince. "You didn't have to. If you don't love him you would have just said no when I asked," he shouted. "Malcolm, why do you wanna go there?"

"I just wanna know the truth; that's all. So did you fuck him yet?"

"I'm not answering that! That's none of your business," I shouted. He was really crossing the line. "Why not, you might as well? He took you to Jamaica for a weekend." "Is this what you called me for, Malcolm?" To get on my damn nerves about somebody else?" I asked. "I just don't wanna be no fool; that's all. I'm in here thinking about you, and you're out there being the next man's ho," he barked.

"Ho! Nigga, if anybody's the ho, it's your cheating no-good ass! You know what, Malcolm, I'ma tell you what you really want to hear! Yes, I went to Jamaica with my friend. No, my bad, my new man. And yes, we had sex! Every day we were there, multiple times! And if you want to know how it was, it was good. Better yet, it was great! He fucked me like I ain't never been fucked in my life! I forgot you even existed. Oh yeah, his dick is waaaaaayyyyyy bigger than yours! Just in case you needed to know that too. He treated me like a woman. Something you never did when we were together. I gave you everything, Malcolm, and you know it, nigga. Now I found someone who's giving me my happiness, and I'm enjoying every single moment of it!"

"Fuck you, bitch!!!" Malcolm angrily shouted before slamming down the telephone.

After getting off the phone with Malcolm, I felt bad about what I said to him. Although he provoked me, I still should have remained calm. Malcolm had a way of getting under my skin like no one else could. The only reason I still put up with all of his bullshit is because he was my first love. And that's something a girl never forgets, but people grow up and grow apart! I will always love Malcolm, but I stopped being in love with him for quite some time. How can a person continue to love someone and not get that same love in return? I don't feel guilty about moving on. I feel rejuvenated. Malcolm would have kept me inside that dark world of his as long as he could. And if it were not for Prince showing me this wonderful new light that exists, I probably would have still been stuck in Malcolm's darkness. I'm so thankful I found my way out!

~~~

Inside of Sonny's Basement, he and his bodyguard, Dwight, were seated at the bar counting stacks of money that lay scattered along the counter.

"How much is that, Dwight?" Sonny asked. "Thirty-thousand in this pile and twenty-five in this one," Dwight said, separating the two piles. "Did you make sure both cameras are working?" Sonny asked. "Yeah, everything is cool, Sonny. I took care of them," Dwight replied. "Good. I need everything to be right for this weekend. Did you get that broken slot machine fixed?" Sonny said. "Yup, this afternoon," Dwight said. "What would I ever do without you, Dwight," Sonny said, as he smiled at his friend. "You know what, you'd probably lose your damn mind," Dwight jokingly said. "And you're probably right," Sonny laughed, playfully punching Dwight on his shoulder.

After Sonny and Dwight finished counting the rest of the money on the counter, they put everything inside a large brown duffle bag. Once Dwight left, Sonny went behind the bar and opened a secret floor safe. Inside the large hidden safe were large stacks of money. The only other person who had knowledge about the concealed safe was, Summer.

Once the money was neatly stacked with all the rest, Sonny locked up everything and went back upstairs to his apartment. Waiting inside his bedroom was an attractive naked young female, who was barely twenty-one. After getting undressed, Sonny eagerly took one Viagra pill and anxiously joined this *Young-Tender-Ronnie* in his bed.

~~~

With Nolan fast asleep in his bedroom, Latoya and Earl were wrapped in each other's arms, sucking each other's lips and tonguing one another down on the living room couch. Wearing nothing but a thin white t-shirt and a pair of spandex shorts, Earl continued to play with Latoya's wet pussy with his free hand. Completely turned on, Latoya couldn't help but enjoy the wonderful sensation she felt flowing throughout her body.

As Earl began sucking on her large erect nipples, Latoya moaned out, enjoying the pleasures of the man she long craved. After sliding down Latoya's shorts, Earl pulled down his sweatpants, displaying his bulky and massive ten-inch dick. Jumping back like a frightened child, Latoya's eyes almost popped from her head at the sight of his enormous penis.

"Whoa! Hold on, Earl. This has gone a little bit too far. I'm sorry. I'm so sorry," Latoya said, pulling her shorts up. "We are moving way, way too fast. I'm sorry. Please don't be mad at me," Latoya said, taking a long, and much needed deep breath from all of the excitement. "I'm not mad at you, Latoya. I understand," Earl said, pulling up his black sweatpants. "Are you sure?" Latoya said, looking into his disappointed eyes.

"I'm positive, Latoya. You're right. Things are going too fast between us. It's just when I'm around you; I can't help but want you. Maybe we should just take a break for a while," Earl suggested. "Earl, please don't be upset. I'm just afraid of being hurt again. That's all," Latoya confessed. "I do understand. And I don't want you to do anything that you'll regret afterward, Latoya."

"Earl, I like you a lot, and I'd like for us to continue to get closer. I just don't want to rush things," she repeated. "Well, I still think we should take a break. I have a lot to think about as well," Earl said, standing up and walking over to the front door. "No goodnight kiss?" Latoya said, walking behind him, feeling the sudden tension.

After giving Latoya a quick kiss on the lips, Earl opened the door and walked out, quickly shutting the door behind him. Sitting back down on the couch, Latoya's mind seemed to be in a state of confusion. As much as Earl turned her on, and as much as she was attracted to him, Latoya knew that sleeping with Earl too soon would be a very big mistake.

After a long sigh of relief, Latoya turned off the TV and went into her lonely bedroom. Lying in her bed, she reached under her pillow and grabbed her trusty vibrator. And once again she began massaging her wet pussy until she peeked; wishing the whole time she could feel the ten-inch beast attached to Mr. Smith.

CHAPTER 9

Thursday Morning

"Hello," Summer said, answering her cell phone while driving to work. "Hey, honey, it's me," Sonny said into the phone. "Daddy, I'll be over later this afternoon to see you. Is everything alright at the bar and the barbershop?" "Everything's fine, sweetie. How are things going with you and Prince?" her father asked. "Wonderful! Absolutely nothing to complain about," she said proudly. "I'm glad that you've found someone who finally makes you happy. Lord knows how many times you've cried over Malcolm. And I can see that you two feel deeply for one another, and that's a beautiful thing," Sonny said.

"Thank you, daddy. I told you Prince was different, and if you gave him a chance you'd like him. Daddy, he reminds me a lot of you. He's smart, loving and overprotective just like you are. Oh, and I can't forget, he's handsome too," Summer said giggling. "So this is the one, huh?" "The only one! I don't have to look any further." "Well, I was always told men pick, and women choose. You remember what I told you, about the two types of people in the world?" her father asked.

"Yes, Daddy. The ones that are going your way and the ones that are in your way. How could I ever forget that?" "Just making sure you didn't," Sonny said, pleased that his child was retaining the knowledge he had shared with her. "Well, if things keep going as they are between you two, then maybe I'll finally get my grandson so he can run my empire when I'm gone," Sonny said. "Maybe. But you aren't going anywhere anytime soon, so please stop saying that," Summer said seriously.

"I always tell you, Summer, that tomorrow ain't guaranteed to no one?" Sonny said. "Daddy, you know I don't like to talk about that stuff," she fussed. "Well, it's the truth! And if anything ever happens to me, you're my only beneficiary. You'll be well taken care of," he said. "I don't care about no money, Daddy, and you know it. Now stop talking like that before I start crying," she said sadly.

"Okay, okay! I'm sorry, sweetie. You know I can't stand to see you cry, so please don't. You're right. I'll just see you later on. Bye, bye," Sonny said. "Bye, bye, Daddy," Summer said, ending the call and pulling into her parking space in front of the salon.

Thinking about what Sonny had just said, Summer sat inside her car wiping away her tears. Whenever her father talked about dying, Summer cried. Death was a reality of life, but it was one of those topics she'd rather not discuss. Sonny was all she had in this world and the thought of him not being around anymore crushed her soul.

Later That Evening

"You're pregnant!" Latoya shouted as Keisha continued to drive to the Y.M.C.A. so they could pick up Nolan. "Yeah. I found out when I went to the clinic for my appointment," Keisha said. "Then why aren't you excited? You always wanted a baby. Boo will be happy," Latoya said. "What if the baby ain't his?" Keisha said. "Latoya, you know I have two other friends besides Boo," she continued.

"What! Girl, stop playing. Don't tell me you don't know who you're pregnant by, Keisha!" Latoya snapped. "I didn't say that. I just said what if it ain't his, and it's one of my other friends."

"Who are these other guys you've been seeing anyway? You better not let Boo find out. You know what happened before when he caught you creeping around and beat you and Mark up. And then he kicked you out of his house and took back the car he bought you. I thought you would never leave Summer's house. And if Boo didn't apologize and come back to get you, you'd still be there now."

"I told Boo that Mark and I were just old friends. He didn't have to embarrass us like that in the movie theater. And Mark can't stand his ass for doing that shit," Keisha said, still trying to act as if she hadn't slept with Mark. "Keisha, who do you think you're talking to? You and Mark were creeping around, on and off for years. Ain't nobody stupid! Is Mark one of those secret lovers of yours?" Latoya asked. "No, it's not Mark's. I haven't seen Mark in a while. Ever since that beat down," Keisha said, flashing a small grin.

"Then who's the father if it ain't Boo or Mark?" Latoya said, demanding an answer. "If I tell you, Toya, promise me you'll keep it between you and me. No one else, just you and me," Keisha said. "Who is it, girl?" Latoya pressed. "No, promise me first. I'm serious, Toya, or else I won't tell you who it is," Keisha said, as she pulled up to the front of the Y.M.C.A., and parked her car.

"Who is it, Keisha?" Latoya asked again, waiting for an answer. After a long deep breath, "It's Sonny! Sonny's the father," Keisha blurted out. "You've been sleeping around with Mr. Sonny? Keisha, what the fuck is wrong with you!

Summer's father? Are you crazy girl?" Latoya said, shaking her head in disbelief. "Things just happened, Latoya," Keisha said.

"Getting pregnant doesn't just happen. It takes two! And you could've used a damn condom. You nasty girl! So that's who you've been creeping around with; leaving the job on your lunch break for Mr. Sonny?"
"Okay, don't keep saying it! I already feel bad enough," Keisha said. "You should! Mr. Sonny has known us since we were both little girls. He's like somebody's dad, Keisha."

"Well, I ain't a kid no more. And I enjoy being with Sonny. And yeah, he's like a Big-Daddy, and I don't feel bad about fucking him! We both grown and I ain't hurting nobody," Keisha said sharply. "Well, you better hope Summer doesn't find out about this. Or Boo's crazy ass."
"Well, how will they know if you and I are the only two people who know about it?" Keisha said.

"I gave you my word, Keisha, but if this shit gets blown wide open, leave me the hell out of it," Latoya said, opening the car door and letting her son, Nolan, inside.

As Keisha started her car back up, both ladies looked at one another and could only shake their heads. This was too much to talk about and for now neither had another word to say.

Manhattan, New York
Inside the Radisson Hotel

"When will you be back in town, Papi?" the beautiful young Latin female said, lying in bed. "In a few weeks, Shakira, I'll be back," Boo said, putting his clothes on.

"Do you want me to bring another girl with me again for the next time?" she asked. "Damn right! I'm addicted now," Boo said. "You just make sure your brother doesn't find out about us sleeping around. He'll snap out if he finds out I was fucking his little sister," Boo said.

"Tonyman ain't my father. I'm nineteen now. I can do what I want! But still, he doesn't need to know everything I do," Shakira said. "Just keep this on the hush, Shakira. Like I said, I'll be back in a few weeks so be ready," Boo commanded. "Ain't I always?" Shakira said, getting out of the bed, showing off her shapely body.

"That's why I fucks with you, Mami because you know how to play your part," Boo said, as he stared at her beautiful body. "And you know how to treat me like a real woman," Shakira said, giving him a seductive look, as she put her black thong on.

"Take care, Shakira. I'll see you soon," Boo said, walking towards the door. "No kiss before you leave, Papi?" "You know I don't kiss on the lips, Shakira," Boo said firmly. "I ain't talking about on your lips," Shakira said, kneeling down on her knees. "You don't have to leave for another half hour. You still have some time to let me enjoy that magic stick," she said, unzipping his jeans and taking out Boo's hard dick.

Standing with his back up against the door, Boo relaxed as Shakira began devouring his dick inside her large, wet mouth. Enjoying every moment, Boo placed his hands on top of her head and fucked her face; taking her throat on the ride of a lifetime.

Chicago
Later That Night
Prince

The windy city reminded me of Philadelphia. The people and the atmosphere were almost the same; except the bitter cold of Chicago was unmatched by any winter's day in Philly.

Chicago's hard ghettos were very similar to those back in Philly. Graffiti covered the walls, and there were abandoned houses and empty lots throughout the urban neighborhoods. And the El-train that ran back and forth across the city was just like the Broad Street Line. So much similarity, I thought as I drove through Lincoln Park en route to the Drake Hotel in downtown Chicago.

For two days and nights, I had been carefully observing this short, stocky white man. I learned his moves from where he liked to eat, to the time where he would sneak away from his wife to see his twenty-something-year-old mistress.

After leaving Maggiano's Little Italy Italian Restaurant, I followed him and his young bunny to the Drake Hotel. Patiently, I waited outside the hotel in my car. Tonight was the night that this old man's life would come to a sudden end. He had no indication that an enemy was nearby. And no way to stop his demise.

As I sat, I watched as the happy smiling couple, who had just enjoyed a wonderful night out, strolled out the front door of the Drake. Parked beside his brand new Cadillac, I was ready and waiting inside my black midsize rental car. As the smiling pair approached their car, I quickly exited my vehicle. Holding a loaded 9mm with an attached silencer, I walked up behind them.

"Don't say a word. Just get in the car," I demanded, catching them off guard. "Just take the money. My wallet is in my pocket," the man frighteningly said. "Just get in the fucking car, man!" I said, putting the pistol to his back.

Cold steel pressed closely to the flesh, often gets me the results I need. After the three of us were inside of his car, I instructed the man to drive off. Scared and confused, he drove down the dark street with his frightened passenger sobbing; as I kept my gun pointed at them while seated in the backseat.

"Park over there," I said when we were only a few blocks away from my vehicle. "Please, take the money! Take the car, just don't kill me," the man begged, as his terrified female associate continued to cry.

"Both of you close your eyes and start counting to a hundred," I demanded. "PLEASE, PLEASE, just take the money!" the man pleaded. "SHUT THE FUCK UP AND DO AS I SAID! Now close your eyes and count," I said, reaching from the backseat and turning up the volume on the radio.

As they began counting with their eyes closed, I pointed my gun at the back of the man's head. Pulling the trigger once, the old man's head slumped down to his chest. It was an instant kill. I then quickly took a photo of the deceased man as the woman continued counting.

"47, 48, 49, 50, 51, 52." The scared young woman continued to count out loud with her eyes shut solid. "99, 100," she said, and by the time she finally opened her watery eyes I was gone. She was left to realize that her old gray-haired sugar daddy had no more life left inside of him. I'm sure the blood, along with the brain splatter sent screams echoing into the night, but I couldn't stick around to see it. By now I had returned to my car and drove away.

"Just two more and it's all over," I said as my reality started to hit me. "Just two more," I said, as my eyes stung from the tears of guilt and shame that flowed from within.

Frackville Prison
Upstate Pennsylvania

"I hate you, bitch! Malcolm said, lying on his bunk staring at Summer's picture. "How the fuck you gonna do me like this? How you gonna give my pussy to some other nigga? I hate you! I hate you! I hate you!" he shouted out.

Grabbing the small razor he had, Malcolm began cutting up the picture. Looking like a possessed demon, he continued to say, "I hate you! I hate you," as he sliced away. Looking down from the top bunk, his cellmate shook his head at the foolish and childish act Malcolm was engaged in.

After spending twenty years in the joint, he had seen this behavior many times. A young man comes in fresh off the streets, crying about his woman leaving him for another man; sometimes another woman. The bad part about it was that most of these men never got over it. Too many let the happenings of the outside world interfere with the time they had left to serve. Lying back on his pillow, he knew Malcolm would be one of the weaker inmates who couldn't handle the fact that another man was loving his woman. He thought about the short amount of time Malcolm had to serve, and it was clear to him that his cellmate would not have it easy as he served his remaining sentence inside of the walls.

Brooklyn, New York

Antonio Sanchez, aka Tonyman, was thirty-five, muscular, 5'10", and had a temper like a stick of pure dynamite. His brown skin looked as if it was permanently kissed by the sun, and his curly, soft light brown hair was tinted with hints of blonde. He had extremely long feet. His shoe size was a fourteen.

In 1995, he and his younger sister, Shakira, left Columbia and moved to the United States. He was his sister's primary caretaker because their parents remained in Columbia.

Tonyman found work quickly. Having risen through the ranks of his Uncle Felix's ruthless drug cartel, he was able to provide fully for his sister and himself. After the FBI had investigated his Uncle Felix and a federal grand jury indicted him, he was immediately taken to Lewisburg Federal Penitentiary, where he was sentenced to spend the rest of his adult life. Now, Tonyman had become the man. He controlled his uncle's corrupt drug organization, supplying two of New York's five boroughs, and parts of New Jersey and Philadelphia as well.

"Shakira, where have you been for the last few days?" Tonyman said, sitting at the living room table with two of his men. "You hear me talking to you, girl," he shouted. "I was at Joy's house in Queens, Tony! Damn," Shakira shouted back. "Next time you're gonna be away for more than a night, you better let me know," he demanded. "I'll be gone all next week. You happy now?" Shakira sarcastically said, walking up the stairs to her bedroom. "It's summer time and I'm not going to be locked in the house all day,"

Shakira yelled, before going into her bedroom and slamming the door behind her.

Shakira was the typical spoiled younger sister who had always gotten what she wanted. And all of Tonyman's gray hairs had come from worrying about his little sister. Tonyman knew people would use, hurt, and manipulate the people he loved most just to get to him. In this cruel and vicious game, his enemies wouldn't hesitate to get hold of the one person who meant the world to him — Shakira, his younger, beautiful sister. So his overprotective ways were only for her safety.

Inside her large pink beautifully decorated bedroom, Shakira laid across her canopy bed. Thinking about the enjoyable time she spent with Boo, a seductive grin appeared on her face. Tonyman wasn't aware that his younger sister was a sexually charged, active teenager; one who not only enjoyed being with older men but women as well. Boo had essentially been the person who turned her on to having sex with women. He had introduced her to her first threesome, and the taste of a woman's pussy in her mouth was like sweet nectar to a honeybee. Shakira enjoyed the touch and tongue of a woman and had no quarrels about returning any and all favors.

Saturday Night
Summer

After receiving Prince's phone call, I couldn't wait to see his face. He said he'd be over shortly, and I couldn't help but run back and forth to the window to see if his blue Mercedes had pulled into my driveway. The time was 8:30

P.M. and the bright full moon had already replaced the fading sun.

As I sat by the window watching ever so attentively as the flow of cars drove up and down the street, the melodic voice of India Arie streamed smoothly from the stereo. Seeing the light drizzling rain slowly falling from heaven brought a lovely smile to my face. There was just something about God's falling tears that had always brought warmth to my soul.

Dressed in an all-black Victoria's Secret teddy, I knew if Prince saw me in this sexy outfit he'd be instantly turned on. And to add to the sexually charged atmosphere, the exotic smell of scented candles roamed throughout the house.

Finally, my long wait had come to an end as I watched Prince pull into the driveway and park. I quickly unlocked the front door and rushed upstairs into my bedroom. After dimming the lights inside, I laid across the bed. Hearing the front door open and shut, filled me with slight anxiety. I heard my man walking upstairs, and his footsteps led him straight to the bathroom; where he undressed and entered the steamy shower, I had running for him.

After exiting from the shower, he dried his body. I patiently waited on top of the bed for him. Verbally I was speechless, but my body had a thousand requests, and Prince would soon have to oblige my demands.

Walking into the bedroom he noticed me in my erotic black lingerie, and I noticed the large bulge growing rapidly as he walked closer to the bed. My plan was working as intended, and I smiled at the thought of what was going to happen next. Prince sat next to me on the bed; he lifted me up, and our tongues met with a long, deep, passion-filled kiss. As one of his hands ran through my hair, the other worked its way down my sensitive spine. Slowly, he began to undress what little I had on. Once I was naked, he gently lay me down on the bed. His long, burly warm tongue now traveled to every curve on my pulsating body. My intense moans filled the faintly lit room, as the rivers began to overflow from my vibrating pussy. His tongue caressed my erogenous zone, as he vivaciously sucked my clitoris.

Reaching under the pillow, Prince pulled out my small but powerful silver vibrator. His tongue created one wonderful sensation, and now the vibrations from the vibrator going across my breasts created a concurrent sensation that was going to cause an explosion. My nails dug deeper into his skin, leaving long scratches across his strong back. My hard moans increased as his tongue moved wilder and faster. I screamed! Yelled! Begging Prince to hurry and fill my thriving utopia with his hard dick. He obliged!!!

As he placed my legs around his waist and entered my drenched womb, my pussy juices covered his large dick each time he stroked. My nails continued to dig into his flesh as our tongues danced in perfect harmony. I could feel my entire body erupting, and passion filled me as Prince continued to make love to me as only he could.

Finally, after a long sweaty, sex-session filled with lust and love, our bodies erupted as we shared powerful orgasms. Too tired to talk we laid in each other's arms, covered in running sweat, as our heartbeats beat rapidly.

"I almost forgot," Prince said softly. "How's my light shining?" he smiled. "As bright as ever knowing that I'll always have you," I said, as we drifted to sleep.

One Hour Later

"Ahhhhhhh!!!!" Prince screamed out, quickly waking Summer from the peaceful sleep she was enjoying. "What's wrong, baby?" she said, seeing her man's face covered in fright and dripping sweat. Nervously shaking, Prince remained silent.

"Baby, what's wrong? Was it a bad dream?" she said, looking into his terrified eyes. "Prince, talk to me," she cried, grabbing his unsteady hands. "Baby, please say something," she said, as tears of uncertainty and panic fell from her eyes. "Did you have a nightmare? Tell me what's wrong! Tell me what's wrong, Prince," Summer said, getting choked up on her words.

"Yes...I had a nightmare. That's all," Prince finally said, coming back to reality. "What was it about? You were really out of it," Summer asked, feeling extremely concerned. "Nothing. It was nothing, baby," Prince said, taking a few long deep breaths. "Something made you scream. What was it, Prince?" Summer asked, trying to get her man to open up to her about the nightmare that caused such a commotion.

"Really, baby, it was nothing. I just had a bad dream. Now let's go back to sleep," Prince said.

As Summer lay down, she knew it was much more than a dream. Something had to be wrong, but Prince wasn't comfortable enough to share it with her. Indeed, something was wrong, and whatever it was it had Prince shaking in his sleep for the rest of the night.

CHAPTER 10

One Week Later
Saturday Evening
Outside the hair salon, Keisha was smoking a cigarette and talking to Latoya.

"So what are you gonna do, Keisha?" Latoya said. "I don't know. I'm still confused about everything," she confided. "Well, if you decide to keep your baby, at least try and find out who's the father," Latoya instructed. "I'm pretty sure who the father is," Keisha said. "So you still think it's Mr. Sonny's huh?" "I'm positive. I just don't know what I'm gonna do and if I should tell him," she said.

"Keisha, Keisha, Keisha, the trouble you get yourself into," Latoya said, shaking her head, feeling sorry for her friend. "I don't wanna hurt Boo," Keisha said, blowing a puff of smoke into the air. "Well, it's too late for that now," Latoya reminded her. "What do you think I should do?" "I don't know, Keisha. I really don't know. Why didn't you make Sonny use a condom?" Latoya asked.

"I did at first. Then after a while, he just stopped. And I never said anything about it because I liked that shit raw," Keisha said. "I think you should tell Summer," Latoya said, looking directly at her friend. "What! No way! She would kill me if she found out that I've been sleeping with her father," Keisha replied. "No, she won't. I think she'll understand. She loves you like a sister," Latoya said, still looking straight in the eyes of her friend.

"And I don't want that to stop," Keisha said looking away from Latoya. "Just think about it. And if you do decide to tell her, do it before you start showing and she finds out anyway. That's what friends do. Tell the damn truth to one another even if it hurts," Latoya said. "What about Boo?" Keisha said, throwing the cigarette butt to the ground and stomping on it. "Now that's someone you have to deal with alone. You can't lie to him to make him believe that that's his baby when it's not, because if he ever finds out the truth, all hell will break loose." Seeing the scared expression on Keisha's face, Latoya put her arms around her friend to provide some comfort.

"Don't worry, Keisha, things will work themselves out. Just ask God to help you get through it and everything will be okay."

As both girls walked back into the salon, a mini smile appeared on Keisha's face. Even with all the drama surrounding her, Keisha still knew she could always count on her two best friends. Now she just had to find the courage to fess up her truth and fix things.

Later That Night
Summer

After watching Floetry and Erykah Badu perform live at the Tower Theater on 69th Street in Upper Darby, PA, Prince and I got into his car and headed back to his place.

"I have something for you," Prince said with a bright smile. "What is it?" I blushed. He always gave the best gifts, so I was excited. "You'll see soon, beautiful," Prince said, as he continued to drive down Market Street.

"Tell me what it is?" I asked as curiosity was killing me. "Be patient! Good things come to those who wait," he said, taunting me. For the rest of the ride, I remained quiet as Prince continued to smile and drive.

Twenty minutes later we arrived at his home. After getting out of the car, Prince grabbed my hand, and I followed him into the building. Inside the elevator, I noticed he pressed the button for the top floor. I knew something was up because Prince's apartment was on the sixth floor.

When the elevator finally stopped, we got off, and I followed him down the quiet, bare hallway. Reaching the stairs that led to the rooftop of the building, Prince grabbed my hand again. I followed him up the short flight of stairs, and he opened the door and walked out onto the rooftop. Seeing two chairs at the small decorated table, with a bottle of champagne and two glasses sitting on top of it, I smiled bright enough to light the sky.

Prince led me over to the table, pulled out my chair, and I took my seat. Sitting directly across from me, Prince reached across the table and grabbed both of my hands.

"Do you like it?" he asked, looking into my watery eyes. I was turning into such the teary eyed romantic. I couldn't respond immediately because I was trying to keep my tears from dripping down. "I guess that means yes," he said, wiping my tears away. Sliding his chair next to mine, Prince continued to look deep into my eyes.

"Prince, why are you doing this to me? Why? Tell me why?" I asked tearfully. "Because you deserve it. And I won't let you become another black woman who missed out on the necessary pleasures of life. That's why I brought you up here tonight," he said. "And why's that? Why are we up here?" I said, looking out at the beautiful downtown skyline.

"Because I wanted to bring you closer to heaven," Prince said. "Yeah, you laying it on thick tonight aren't you," I asked. "Just thick enough for you to fall in love with me a little more," he said, as his lips met mine.

Prince stood me up and walked behind me. He bent me over, and I held onto the table as Prince slid down my thong and lifted up my Dolce & Gabbana dress. Seconds later, I felt his hard dick thrust deep inside of me as he momentarily quenched my pussy's never ending desire for him.

Tonight, we made love in the company of the bright shining stars and under the full yellow moon that watched us from high above. Loving this man felt so good!

~~~

Sonny's Basement was overcrowded with all its regular Saturday night gamblers. As Sonny sat on a stool talking to the beautiful young bartender behind the counter, Dwight, his trusted bodyguard, stood by the door checking everyone who came in. Just moments earlier, Sonny had thrown a man out for switching his loaded dice at one of the crap tables, and Dwight had to break up a dispute between two females who started fighting over one of the slot machines.

As Sonny continued to sweet talk this gorgeous young female, a loud crash through the door startled them both. Seeing two masked men holding guns in their hands had everyone in complete shock. One of the men had his gun pointed at Dwight, while the other one walked straight up to Sonny. Everyone stood around with their hands in the air. No one said a word as the masked man gripped Sonny and forced him around the counter.

"Open the safe, old man!!!" he demanded. "I don't know what you're talking about," Sonny said, staring down the barrel of the 45. "Move out of the way, bitch!" the man yelled out to the scared bartender who was standing there crying.

As she hurried off, the masked men again said to Sonny, "Open the damn safe!!!" "I said, I don't know what you're talking about," Sonny calmly said, once more. "Move out of the way, old man," the man said, as Sonny stepped back. Looking on the floor, he noticed a small hole. After putting his finger inside the hole, the masked man pulled up the piece of wood. Beyond that large piece of wood was a safe containing over a million dollars of Sonny's money.

"Jackpot!!!" the man yelled out to his partner who was still by the door pointing his gun at Dwight's head. Taking the large black sports bag from around his shoulder, the man began putting stacks of money inside of it. As he loaded up his bag, Sonny was slowly easing backward to get his loaded 357, which he kept hidden by the cash register. Seeing Sonny reaching for something, the man suddenly stood up. As Sonny turned and pointed his 357, the man unloaded two bullets into Sonny's chest. Sonny fell to the floor. The masked man left the rest of the money in the safe, grabbing his bag and quickly ran off. Rushing through the crowded basement of shocked onlookers, the masked men rushed out of the door. Dwight ran behind them and watched as the two jumped into a dark car and pulled off with a getaway driver who had been waiting for them.

There was no way Dwight could apprehend the men, so he rushed back inside. He closed the safe and placed the floorboard down so no one could see Sonny's stash spot. As Dwight turned his attention to his friend, it was clear he wasn't doing well. Dwight held Sonny in his arms and sobbed.

"Call an ambulance," he yelled out loud. "Somebody call an ambulance," he said, seeing Sonny's blood gush out from his chest as it covered his white shirt.

After the ambulance arrived and took Sonny to the nearby hospital, Dwight and many patrons gave statements to the cops. Dwight told the officers that three masked men had stolen money from the cash register. Since no one had seen the safe and didn't know it existed, they took his word. When the detectives finished their final questioning, Dwight closed up the Basement and called Summer's cell phone.

Dwight struggled to tell Summer what had just happened to her father, but he found a way to get it out. Summer and Prince rushed to the hospital. Summer's eyes were saturated with tears, and her heart ached, as she sat nervously inside of the hospital's waiting room. Dwight and Prince were beside her, as Keisha and Latoya walked through the door. Quickly, both girls ran to her side, collapsing into one another's arms. Dwight stood up, pacing back and forth, and Prince tried to remain strong as he felt every bit of his woman's pain. Leroy, Sonny's young friend was there too. He sat in a chair with his head buried in his hands crying.

An hour later, a tall, lanky, pale-faced, Caucasian doctor with a long pointy nose walked into the waiting room and asked for Summer. His thick brown framed glasses barely stayed on his face, as he repositioned his lab coat. He escorted Summer into the hallway alone as he delivered the news he had about her father.

Everyone inside the waiting room heard the loud maddening screams as Summer cried out in agony. Sonny was dead! Running into the hallway, Prince grabbed his grieving woman into his protective arms. Dwight shook his head while Keisha and Latoya held each other crying.

"He's gone!!! He's gone!!! My father is gone, Prince!!! Somebody killed my father," Summer tearfully shouted out. "They killed him!!! They killed my father!!! They killed my father," Summer continued to cry. As Prince held her tight in his arms, all Summer could think about was losing her father. She had lost her mother, and now both of her parents were gone. All she had left in this harsh and unkind world was Prince.

Prince

After leaving the hospital that night, I drove Summer back home. All night long we cried together in each other's arms. I knew exactly how it felt to lose someone so close after losing my mother a few years ago. I never knew my father, but losing a parent is as painful as anything a child can experience.

Sitting up on the sofa, Summer looked deep into my watery eyes. "Prince, promise me that you'll never leave me," she said, as her tears continued to fall from her sorrow filled face. "Promise me that you'll never go away from me," she said. I grabbed her face and looked straight into her eyes. "I promise you. I'll be here for you, and I'm not going anywhere. These aren't words without truth behind them. This is a promise from my heart to yours. I will never leave you," I said, as she wrapped herself back into my arms and cried herself to sleep.

The Next Day
Inside A House On 42nd & Mantua Avenue
West Philadelphia

"What the fuck happened," Dwight screamed out at the three nervous young men. "Man, he was reaching for his gun. I had to shoot him," one of the men said. "I told you, Dillon, that no one was supposed to get hurt! I specifically told you that," Dwight barked. "Uncle Dwight, what was I supposed to do, just let Sonny shoot me?" he asked.

"Uncle, Dillon is right. He had to shoot Sonny or Sonny would have shot him," another one of the men said, looking at all the stacks of money on the table. "We didn't need any blood on our hands. And I didn't want Sonny to die," the backstabbing Dwight said. "Sometimes things happen that we have no control over. It was you who set this all up, Uncle Dwight. You're the one who told us about his secret safe he had in the Basement. And you made sure the cameras weren't working. We only did as we were told," Dwight's nephew Perry said.

"I know, Perry, but I never said anything about killing Sonny," Dwight said, shaking his head. "I'm sorry your friend had to die, Unc, but still, it was either his life or Dillon's," Perry continued. "You said your friends down at the station didn't find anything, right?" his other nephew Courtney said.

"So far, Courtney, they don't have anything. All they know is a robbery took place, and a man was killed. But Sonny has a lot of friends who care about him, so we still have to be very careful that no one ever finds out about this. Do Y'all hear me?" Dwight said sternly. "Yes, Uncle Dwight, we hear you," Dillon said, taking his share of the money from off the table.

"Four hundred and thirty-three thousand dollars!!! We need to be celebrating," Perry said, as everyone smiled except Dwight.

After everyone had taken their hundred thousand dollar cut, Dwight took the rest of the money and left. Driving his car, Dwight thought about his good friend, Sonny. He was deeply saddened that he had been the mastermind behind the robbery that led to Sonny's tragic murder.

As he stopped at a red light, his guilt filled tears raced from is deceptive eyes. To compose his racing nerves, he lit a cigarette to calm down. Turning up the volume on the radio as loud as he could to block his shameful thoughts, he pulled off.

"All I wanted was the money, Sonny," he said to himself as he drove. "Why couldn't you just give up the money! Why couldn't you just give up the damn money," Dwight yelled, slamming his right fist down hard on the steering wheel?

After working with Sonny for over twenty years, Dwight never imagined that one day he and his three devious nephews would all play a part in the killing of his good friend, Sonny Jones.

CHAPTER 11

One Week Later
Pinn Memorial Baptist Church
54th Street

"Will that be all?" the Pastor asked the large crowd of grieving friends and relatives. "Does anyone else wish to say any other final farewells to this gentleman that God has called back home?" he continued. "I would. I have something to say, sir," Prince said, standing up from his seat next to Summer.

As everyone hearts bled and tears filled their grief-stricken eyes, Prince approached the podium and grabbed the microphone. "I have a poem that I would like to read. It's called, *A Moment*," he said, before beginning.

How could you ever know pain if you've never felt its wrath?
Why does God take away those who bring us joy and make us laugh?
Tell me why is true happiness so hard to find?
And through the process of attaining it, many lose their minds.
Why can't we all enjoy this wonderful light that God has placed in our hearts?
Why are so many people still caught up in this life, unable to escape the dark?
Why are we all grieving instead of smiling and laughing?
Why do we shed a million tears from seeing another black man passing?
I'm telling y'all today that it can all go in a blink of an eye.
We have a moment to be born, and a moment to die.

A moment to love and understand. A moment to truly feel alive.
So please find your moment as we wait for our God to arrive.

"Thank you," Prince said, as he finished and walked back over to his seat next to Summer. Sitting in the row directly behind them, Keisha was crying heavily in Boo's arms. Latoya sat in between her son, Nolan, and Earl. Dwight couldn't sit. He stood in the back of the church holding Sonny's obituary in his hands, crying with Leroy.

Prince

After the funeral and burial had ended, Summer, Latoya, Keisha, and I drove back to Summer's house. As the four of us talked in the living room, Keisha asked to speak with Summer in private. Leaving Latoya and me inside the living room, Summer and Keisha went upstairs into her bedroom and shut the door behind them.

"What's going on?" I asked Latoya, making sure that Summer and Keisha were okay. "Keisha has something important to tell Summer," Latoya said. "Do you know what it is?" I asked, concerned that too much had already taken place in Summer's day. "Don't worry, Prince, you'll find out soon," Latoya said.

~~~

"What's up, Keisha?" Summer said, taking a seat on the bed. Keisha sat beside her grieving best friend and then looked into Summer's heartbroken eyes. "I have something to tell you, Summer. It has been bothering me, and I think it's best that you know."

"What is it?" Summer asked concerned. "You know how lately I've been leaving the shop on my lunch break," Keisha said. "Yeah, how can I not know? You're gone for an hour," Summer said, slightly smiling. "Well, I've been seeing someone. Someone that I care about and truly love," Keisha confessed. "Duh, it doesn't take a rocket scientist to know that you're out doing your thing behind Boo's back," Summer said.

"Well, that's why I needed to talk to you, Summer," Keisha said, as the butterflies grew in her tiny pregnant filled belly. "Is something wrong, Keisha?" Summer said, grabbing Keisha's hand. "I'm pregnant, Summer... I found out at my last doctor's appointment," she blurted out.

"Wow. Yeah, that's something to tell. Is it Boo's?" Summer asked curiously. "No. Boo is not my baby's father," Keisha replied. "Then who is the father?" Summer inquired. "It's Sonny. Sonny Jones is the father of my child," Keisha said, as a single tear fell from her left eye. "My father! You were sleeping with my father, Keisha?" Summer said confused, as she tried to process the information she had just received. "I'm sorry, Summer, but after that night you took me to the Basement things just started happening. And one thing just led to another. Sonny didn't want to tell you. He never wanted to hurt you and neither did I. I cared about Sonny, Summer. That's why I'm keeping my baby," Keisha said, swallowing hard now that she realized she had just given her friend a lot of information to digest.

"Keisha, you could have come to me and told me. I knew my father liked you, and I know how much you like older men. I wouldn't have been mad. My father lived his life, and even if I wanted to, I couldn't stop him from seeing you. You know how my father can...could be," Summer said, as her eyes watered remembering that she now had to refer to her father in past tense. "I'm sorry that I just didn't tell you, Summer. I feel so bad. We have been best friends since we were little. I just didn't know how to tell you that I was messing with your dad," Keisha said, as the two embraced momentarily.

"Does Boo know you're pregnant?" Summer asked, getting back to the seriousness of Keisha's dilemma. "No, I haven't told him yet, but I will have to soon. I'm just scared. You know how crazy Boo can get at times. I honestly don't know what he will do when he finds out that the baby isn't his," Keisha said, feeling nervous. "Well, you can't keep him in the dark, or else it will just get worse. And no matter what, Keisha, I'll be right here for you. You just take care of my little brother or sister," Summer said, giving Keisha a long comforting hug.

"Thank you so much, Summer. Thank you. I really didn't know what to do. And after what happened to Sonny, I just knew I had to tell you about our child. Thank you for being a friend. I can't imagine how you are standing so strong, but I'm here for you too. I have your back," Keisha said. "Don't worry, Keisha, everything will be alright. And I'm not as strong as I look...," Summer said, as she burst out into tears and the two cried in each other's arms.

Summer

That night the four of us sat in the living room talking, remembering all the good times that we had shared with my father. Keisha and Latoya were the two sisters that I never had. Growing up, I never felt like an only child because I always had my two best friends around. And Prince was the blessing that God knew I now needed. Right now I couldn't ask for a better support system.

After Keisha and Latoya left and went home, Prince and I remained cuddled in each other's arms on the sofa. Looking at Prince made me miss my father even more. I truly believed God brought Prince into my life to fill the painful void of losing my father. Though no one could ever replace my daddy, Prince's presence alone made matters a lot easier to handle. Knowing that I could always count on Prince to be around made the unsettling feelings shrink inside of me.

God had taken away one great man and brought another great man into my life. I'm a firm believer that everything happens for a reason. So I try to never question God's decisions. My father lived a good long life. The kind of life that only he would want to live. He made no excuses for how he did things; he was simply Sonny. And although he's not around anymore, his loving spirit will always live through me.

Later that night, as I wrapped my body inside Prince's arms, the tears came back as if they had never left. The thought of being in this cruel world alone had entered my mind. Suddenly, Prince woke up from his sleep and noticed my eyes were packed with tears.

"Don't worry, Summer. Baby, you'll always have me," he said. "How did you know that's what I was thinking?" I said in a shocked voice. "Because I know my woman," he said. "I know what makes you smile and what makes you laugh and cry. I know everything your soul desires," he said, as he leaned over and gave me a kiss before wiping away my tears with his hand. "I could never take your father's place, but I will do everything in my power to make him smile down on us from heaven," Prince said.

"I love you, Prince. I love you so much," I said, cuddling closer into his arms.

I don't know why, but at that very moment, I felt like my father was close by. There was a cool draft that lingered near my body, and I could feel his presence. As we fell asleep in each other's arms, even in my dreams, I could feel my father's spirit still upon us.

Early the next morning, I drove over to my father's barbershop. After sitting inside of my car for about twenty minutes, I finally gathered the courage to go inside. Standing in the middle of the floor, I stared at the walls. I looked around at all of the pictures of the famous folks who had been at the shop; entertainers like Sammy Davis, Jr. and Morgan Freeman. Sports athletes such as Jim Brown, Dr. Jay, and Charles Barkley; and singers Marvin Gaye, The Stylistics, and Boyz II Men had been there as well. I then walked over and took down a photo of my father and me. I was around ten-years-old at the time, and I was dressed like a little boy sitting on my father's lap. My father had always wanted a son and thinking about all of the boyish things we did together brought a smile to my face. There were fishing trips, basketball and football games. Then his favorite, boxing matches. He loved going to the fights down at the Blue Horizon or in Atlantic City. So whenever a major bout was in town, I'd be right by his side cheering and shouting for his favorite fighter to win.

"Summer...Summer," the voice called out to me. "Whoa! You scared me," I said, startled at first before realizing it was Leroy. "Well, I was calling you. You were in a daze," Leroy said. "What are you doing here today? You don't start until tomorrow?" I said, putting the picture back up on the wall. "I know. I just came by to clean up a little and get things ready. Summer, I want to thank you again for letting me manage the shop. I promise you that I'ma take care of things just like Sonny would have. And you don't have to worry about me being at work on time or closing up. I'll take care of everything. Just like your father did. I promise," Leroy professed.

"I know you will, Leroy. That's why I gave you the job. My father loved your crazy behind," Summer said, as she smiled and took a seat in one of the barber chairs. "And I loved him too, Summer. He was like the father I never had. I'll never forget Sonny as long as I live. Your father will always be a part of me," Leroy said, sitting down in one of the barber chairs next to her.

For about an hour, Leroy and I sat around reminiscing about my father. We smiled, laughed and cried. I knew that people died and moved on from this earth, but when you love someone as deeply as I loved my father, it's hard to let go...and I don't think I ever will.

CHAPTER 12

Three Days After Sonny's Funeral

Standing over top of the bruised and battered Keisha, Boo continued to smack her in the face. "Bitch, how you gonna play me like this," Boo shouted, as he slapped Keisha hard to the floor. Boo had a crazed angry look plastered on his face, and he demanded an answer. "I gave you everything, you no-good bitch! Everything! But like they say, once a ho always a ho!"

"Fuck you, Ronald!" Keisha said, calling him by his government name. "I fuckin' hate you! Look at what you're doing to my face," Keisha screamed. "Bitch, fuck your face!!!" Boo said, smacking her again.

Grabbing a handful of Keisha's hair, Boo pulled out his loaded 9mm and placed it to her forehead. "I should kill your stinking ass," Boo said, watching as a stream of tears fell down Keisha's terrified face. "Just get all your shit and get the fuck out before I fuckin' kill you, you whore!!! And you better not touch a damn thing I bought," Boo angrily yelled. "Fuck you, bitch, and the fuckin' bastard you're carrying!!!"

Badly beaten and bruised, Keisha managed to get up from the floor. With the looming thought that Boo might kill her, Keisha quickly ran into the bathroom and locked the door. Looking at her swollen face and all the dark contusions on her neck, face, and arms, the tears continued to fall from her sore eyes. Shaking and scared, Keisha didn't know what to do. She had decided to tell Boo the truth about being pregnant with Sonny's child. And instantly the rage filled Boo's mind, and he snapped out.

"Bitch, I want you out of my fuckin' house now! If you don't come from out of this bathroom in one minute, I'ma knock the fuckin' door off the hinges and finish beating your whorey ass!!!" Boo yelled.

Knowing that Boo words were not merely threats and that he'd make good on them, Keisha unlocked the door and rushed out. Running past Boo down the stairs, she went straight out of the front door and never turned back; leaving everything she owned behind.

~~~

"Hello, who is it?" Earl said, picking up the telephone by his bed and turning down the volume on the television. "Hey, it's me, Latoya," she said softly. "Hey, Toya, what's up?" Earl said, now sitting up on his bed. "I just wanted to see how you were doing. Are you busy right now?" Latoya asked. "No, not really. What's up?" he wondered. "I have a surprise for you. Can you come upstairs?" she asked, nicely. "What is it?" Earl asked. "Just come upstairs and find out for yourself. I'll leave my door open. Bye," Latoya said, hanging up.

After putting his clothes on, Earl walked upstairs to Latoya's apartment. Remembering that she had left the door open, he walked inside. Seeing Latoya seated alone on the sofa, he sat down beside her.

"What's up? What's this surprise you have for me?" Earl curiously asked, seeing the big fat smile on Latoya's face. "My son is spending the night at his grandmother's," she said. "So what's up? You want to watch a movie or something?" Earl said, not too excited about watching television when he could have stayed home and done that. "No, tonight I want to be in the movie," Latoya said, passing Earl the condom she had in her hand.

Earl was shocked, and the expression on his face didn't hide it. Earl paused for a moment as he realized what he had long desired was now moments away, and then he smiled. Grabbing the stunned Earl by his hand, Latoya led her 6' 5" chocolate stallion into her cozy bedroom. After cutting off the bright lights, Latoya took off her oversized white t-shirt and laid her naked body across the bed. Reaching over to the CD player, she pressed the play button. The voice of Lizz Wright gracefully cruised through the air.

"Are you sure you're ready, Latoya?" Earl said, taking off his jeans and t-shirt. "I've never been more ready. I know exactly what I want," Latoya said, lying back on the pillow as she caressed her 36D breasts. Looking at Earl's tall, slim but muscular body Latoya became wet from the anticipation of his touch. And seeing his long ten-inch dick made her desire Earl more than ever before.

"It's been a while. I want it all, but can you take your time with me?" Latoya said, staring at his long dark, thick nightstick. "Yes, I will," Earl said, joining her in bed as he climbed on top of Latoya's naked, curvaceous body.

"Aren't you forgetting something?" Latoya said, stopping him dead in his tracks. "What? I got the condom on," Earl said. "I'm not talking about the condom. You don't think you're gonna put that big ass thing inside of me without getting me right, do you?" Latoya said, spreading her legs apart. "Oh, I'm sorry. Yeah, you did say you know exactly what you want," Earl said, as he started kissing on Latoya's soft large breasts.

Latoya laid back enjoying Earl's warm, wet lips on her breasts. He then slowly worked his way down to her shaved pussy. With Latoya's legs wrapped around his shoulders, Earl slowly massaged her clit with his long rotating tongue. When he stuck his tongue deep inside of her pussy, it was as if he had just pressed the button on a water fountain, as her juices saturated his tongue. Enjoying every moment, Latoya moaned and squealed, as her body reacted to the long overdue endeavor of pleasure.

As Latoya rapidly came inside of Earl's mouth, she begged him to penetrate her born again virgin pussy. She had soaked his face, and her pussy was in dire need of all ten of his inches.

Earl was happy to oblige her. He wanted to feel her moist, warm walls just as badly as she wanted him to meet them. As Latoya held onto the brass bedpost, Earl put her legs up on his shoulders and slowly entered her wet inviting pussy. Feeling every single inch of his large, thick, solid, rock hard dick, Latoya felt as if her insides were being ripped apart. But this was the only way she liked it. Long, hard and rough.

Latoya matched stroke for stroke, as she went head to head with her towering Mandingo warrior. And even though Earl's large dick took a moment to get used to, because she hadn't had any dick in a while, let alone a pipe of this size; the pain never felt so good.

Summer

"Just come get me," Keisha said, standing at the pay phone crying. "I'm on my way now. I'll be right there, Keisha," I said, putting my puppy, Love, on the floor. "What's up?" Prince asked, waking up from his sleep. "Boo just beat Keisha up and threw her out of his house. I have to get her. She's at some pay phone by a gas station on Broad Street," I said, as I got out of bed and got dressed. "Do you want me to go with you?" Prince said. "No, I'll be alright. Besides, I don't think she'll want to see you right now. It's embarrassing. Bad enough I have to see her, but I know she won't want anyone else to see her right now. I'll be back soon. Just try and go back to sleep," I said. "Are you sure? I can get dressed and go with you," my caring man said. "No, I'll be alright, baby," I said, kissing Prince on the lips and rushing to get dressed.

Pulling into the gas station on Broad and Lehigh, Keisha saw me and quickly ran over and got into my car. Looking at her bruised swollen face, I couldn't believe that Boo had done that to her. Her tan Gap shirt was covered with blood from her busted lip and nose. Her left eye was as large as a Georgia peach, and all of her long manicured nails were broken.

As she cried on my shoulders, I leaned over and gave her a long hug. I hurt so badly for her, and I didn't want to let her go. I felt so sorry for Keisha. And at that moment, hatred filled my heart. Boo had disgusted me by putting his hands on my friend. My father used to tell me that it's not good to hate anyone, but that's what I felt as I looked at my best friend's battered face.

"Don't worry, Keisha, you'll be okay," I said, trying my best to console her. "He's gonna get his! I swear on my unborn child, Summer! That nigga is gonna pay for what he did to my face! I swear," Keisha said, crying and shaking nervously in her seat. "Don't worry about it. What comes around goes around. God don't like ugly," I said, pulling off and driving down Broad Street.

"That motherfucker put a gun to my head!!! He could have killed me," Keisha yelled. "Calm down, Keisha; everything is going to be alright! Boo can't hurt you no more. It's over now. He ain't nothing but a damn coward who beats up on women," I said. "Summer, I'ma get his ass! He knows I know a lot of shit about him. A lot," Keisha screamed out. "Yeah, but two wrongs don't make a right, Keisha," I said, passing her some tissues from out of my purse.

"Fuck dat! Look at my eye. Fuck Boo!!! I mean it, Summer! His ass is gonna get his! His bitch ass is lucky I ain't got no brothers. Fuck Boo! Fuck his car and fuck his house," Keisha fumed. "Well, you know you can stay in the extra bedroom as long as you want. Just cool out for a while, Keisha. At least until your face heals back up. And stop worrying about Boo. He'll get what's coming to him," I said, as we sat at the red light waiting for it to change.

Seeing the angry, vindictive look on Keisha's face, I knew that she was dead serious about getting Boo back for what he had done to her. Keisha was a sweet girl, but if someone crossed her, a switch turned, and her heart would turn to stone. And Boo was no exception.

After the light had changed green, I pulled off. I watched as Keisha put her head down and started crying again. Seeing my girlfriend in this current state had also brought tears to my eyes. There was just too much going on. I didn't know how to handle it all and for now the only talking I could do was through my tears.

~~~

"Ohh!!! Ohh!!! Oh, Please, don't stop!!! I'm about to cum again," Latoya yelled out, as Earl bent her over the bed fucking her from behind. As her hands gripped the blanket for support, Earl continued to penetrate Latoya's sore wet pussy deeply. Slamming hard against her perfectly rounded ass with each long stroke, her hard moans escaped her mouth. "Fuck me!!! Fuck me!!! Yeah, yeah!!! Don't stop!!! Please don't stop!!!" she begged.

Earl heard her request and continued to fuck her just the way she liked. Turning Latoya around, he put both of her arms around his neck as he lifted her body up from the bed. Standing up, with Latoya wrapped around him like a pretzel, Earl fucked her while carrying her around the small bedroom. Stopping in front of the tall mirror on the wall, Latoya watched as Earl's long hard dick went in and out of her pussy.

"Yes!!! Yes!!! Ummm!!! Ohhh!!!" Latoya shouted as she held on tightly to her human-rollercoaster. "Is this how you like it! Is this how you like to be fucked!" Earl said, talking nasty, as he carried her back and forth across the room. "Yes, Daddy!!! Fuck me!!! Fuck me, Daddy, just like this!!! Yes!!! Yes!!! Daddy!!!" Latoya screamed out loudly as a powerful orgasm took over her body. She thought it was over, but Earl had just gotten started. He bent her back over the bed and fucked her senseless.

CHAPTER 14

Later That Night
Summer

I had just gotten off the telephone with Latoya. After filling her in about Keisha and promising her everything was okay, she couldn't wait to tell me about the superb night she had enjoyed with Earl. Keisha was in the other bedroom talking to someone on my cell phone, who she said was important. As Love and I sat on my bed watching another one of those dumb reality TV shows, my house phone rang.

"Hello," I answered. "How's my light shining?" Prince said. "As bright as ever, knowing I'll always have you," I said, happy to hear from my man. "You miss me?" he asked. "To death," I said, feeling frustrated that he had to leave at a moment's notice and was gone before I got back home.

"How long will you be in Cleveland?" I said. "I'll be back soon. I should have things wrapped up by Friday. Where's Love?" he said. "Right here, missing her daddy," I said, rubbing her back. "She'll keep you company while I'm away. How's Keisha doing?" he asked, genuinely concerned. "She's doing much better. She's still upset, but she'll get through it. That girl is a soldier. She's in her room talking to somebody on the phone."

"That's good to hear," Prince said. "What are you doing right now?" I said, wishing I could be inside of his comforting, warm, strong arms. "I'm inside my lonely hotel room watching TV," he replied. "What are you watching?" "Some dumb reality TV show. What's so funny?" Prince said, hearing me laugh.

"I'm watching the same stupid ass show. What is this world coming to?" I said as we burst out laughing. For the rest of the night, Prince and I remained on the telephone, until we finally fell asleep with our phones still in our hands.

Thursday Morning

The sun shined throughout the city as the temperature rose into the high 90s. Philadelphia was known for its bitterly cold winters and its blistering hot summers. Today the heat was on hell as the city's residents did their best to keep cool. Inside the Hillside Cemetery, Dwight parked his car and walked over to Sonny's tombstone. Laying a yellow rose on top of Sonny's grave, Dwight fell to his knees sobbing. For weeks, his conscience had been killing him, and his guilt was eating him alive.

As his tears fell, he put his hands on Sonny's large tombstone. "I'm so sorry, Sonny! Please forgive me," he yelled out into the empty cemetery. "I needed the money, man, but I didn't want you to die over it! I should have just come to you and told you I was deep in debt and about to lose my house. Now look what I've done! Ever since Helen died from throat cancer, I've been in a financial slump. I spent so much money trying to pay for her treatment and alternative medicine that I had to get a second mortgage on the house. I fucked up man! I swear I didn't want this to happen. Sonny, please forgive me! Please," Dwight yelled.

Getting up from off his knees, Dwight walked over to his car. With his face soaked with sorrows and from the sweltering heat, he drove away.

~~~

"What's up?" Keisha said, talking into the phone. "Uh huh, yeah, around nine is fine. Bye, baby," she said, hanging up the telephone and laying back in bed with a big grin on her swollen face. "You ain't the only muthafucka with connects," Keisha said softly.

Summer's Hair Salon
Summer

"Your stomach feel better?" I said, being sarcastic. "Much better," Latoya said, putting on her apron with a smile so wide it could be seen in New York. "But I don't know how I'll feel tomorrow. King Kong is coming back over tonight," Latoya said, as we laughed ourselves silly. Our clients Tamika and Robin looked at us like we were crazy. They had no idea why we were laughing, but we sure did!

Walking over to the door, I picked up the mail the mailman had just dropped off. With the handful of letters in hand, I walked into my office in the back of the salon. Going through the mail, I came across an unexpected letter. It was from Malcolm. As I opened up the letter, I sat down at my desk and started reading.

Dear Summer,

First, I apologize for what happened the last time we talked on the phone. I'm just so fucking frustrated being locked away like a caged animal. I'm sorry about what happened to your father. Even though he never really liked us being together, I still admired Sonny and looked up to him. When Boo told me what happened, my heart dropped knowing the pain you were going through. I just wanted to write you, Summer, and tell you that I still love you. If this

Prince guy is making you happy now, then I'm happy for you. I had my chance, and I fucked it up. I let the most beautiful woman I've ever known slip right through my hands. They say when you snooze, you lose. I slept! I know I wasn't the best boyfriend in the world, Summer, and I always put the streets and my so-called friends before you. But I honestly did love you. And I still do. And always will. My well has run dry and I'm missing my water, but I brought this thirst on myself.

I just want to thank you for putting up with all my shit for as long as you did. And for getting me out of jail every time I got locked up and helping pay for my lawyer. That stuff I'll never forget as long as I live. The Bible speaks about a woman like you. Proverbs, Ch. 31, verse 10-31. Read it. I think you'll like it. Anyway, you'll continue to be in my prayers. With this time I have, I'ma get my mind right and do what's good. Thanks for the money you sent me. I thought it would stop coming after our last conversation. Then again, I should have known who I was dealing with. You're truly one of a kind, Summer. I hope you get everything you want and wish for, and this guy, Prince, knows that he truly has a real jewel in his possession.

Once again, I'm sorry about your dad. You'll always have a friend in me. Keep your head up, Summer, and remember that it gets greater later.

Love always, Malcolm

My time with Malcolm had ended, my father was gone, and Prince was now my present and future. I needed a moment to gather my thoughts and emotions before going back on the floor.

43rd Street
West Philly

Seeing Boo pull up in front of his apartment, Cheeze quickly got inside of his silver Range Rover. "What's up, nigga," Boo said, shaking his hand. "You get that money from Kenny?" Boo said, pulling off down the street. "Yeah, I got it," Cheeze said, passing Boo the large brown paper bag that he had in his hand. "How much is it?" Boo said, feeling the weight on it. "Seven thousand. He said he'll have the other three later tonight," Cheeze said.

"Make sure you get it from him, Cheeze. I'm trying to have all of Tonyman's money by Saturday when I go to New York. Business is business," Boo smiled, saying his famous one-liner. "He'll have it, Boo," Cheeze said, putting a Tupac song on the radio.

As the music blasted out of the speakers, Cheeze and Boo nodded their heads to the enjoyable and relatable lyrics.

Downtown Cleveland, Ohio

Inside Morton's Restaurant, Prince watched very intensely, as he observed the man from Victor's photo and one of his bodyguards eating and talking at their table. As Prince ate his well-done rib-eye steak, he noticed the old white Russian man get up from his seat and head towards the restroom. Standing guard, his huge bodyguard waited outside of the door.

Seeing that his bodyguard was easily distracted by the attractive tall blonde haired female he was now talking to, Prince made his move. Walking past the two of them as they laughed, Prince entered the bathroom. Looking under the stalls, Prince paused when he saw the black Cole Hann shoes he was looking for. Two other men were using the urinals. Prince walked to the front of the stall where the old man was inside sitting on the toilet. When the older men had finished using the urinals, they hurried back to their tables, leaving the restroom without washing their hands.

Knowing his moment had arrived, with a quick and strong kick to the stall door, Prince burst into the stall. The old helpless man's shocked facial expression was frozen onto his face, as Prince quickly unloaded two silent bullets into the front of his dome. Prince calmly walked over to the sink and washed his hands. After drying them with a paper towel, he walked out of the door and right past the bodyguard and his attractive female associate.

Prince went back to his table and left enough cash to cover his tab and a tip, and then he walked to his car.

"One more, just one more and it's all over," Prince said, getting inside of his black rental car and pulling off down the street. "Just one more," he said, taking a long deep breath. "One more."

Later That Evening

Inside the 16th district police station on Lancaster Avenue, in West Philadelphia, Dwight sat down at one of his co-worker's desk writing a letter. After he had finished, he left the letter on top of the desk and walked away. Walking down the hall, he approached two officers who were talking in the lobby.

"Larry, do you have a minute?" Dwight said, with a perplexed look on his face. "Sure, Dwight, what's up?" Larry said. "There's an important letter on your desk. I think you need to read it," Dwight said with urgency. "Do you know who it's from?" Larry asked cautiously. "You'll find out. Just go read it," Dwight said.

"You need to cheer up, Dwight. You haven't been yourself for the last few weeks. Listen, you retire in less than thirty days. You should be celebrating," Larry said, patting Dwight on the back. "I'll see what this letter is about right now, but I'm serious, Dwight, you need to loosen up a little," Larry said.

As Larry walked down the hall to his desk, Dwight went inside of the empty bathroom. Reaching his desk, Larry picked up the handwritten letter from Dwight. Reading the detailed letter, Larry's mouth dropped, and his heart paused. Dwight had just admitted, in writing, about his participation in the murder of his best friend, Sonny Jones. He not only confessed his sins but he implicated his three nephews as well.

Larry was in total disbelief. Then a loud sound from a single gunshot rang out from the men's bathroom. As his fellow officers raced to see what was going on, Larry remained at his desk; wiping his eyes because he knew what had just occurred.

Inside of the bathroom, the group of police officers were perplexed. On top of the toilet, Dwight's body was slumped over with a .38-bullet lodged inside his brain. His .38-revolver lay on the floor by his feet. Less than thirty days before his retirement from the force, Dwight's guilty conscious had taken over him. "A life, for a life," was the final sentence in his confession letter. Dwight had kept his promise.

CHAPTER 15

42nd & Mantua Avenue

Several white and blue police cars were parked outside the row house. Barricades blocked off the street to the many spectators. While flashing lights engulfed the block, little children watched the scene on their bicycles, while the nosey elders watched from their porches. Inside the small row home, Courtney, Perry, and Dillon loaded their weapons and were ready for war.

"Come out with your hands up in the air," an officer yelled through the bullhorn. "Fuck you," a voice said, as a barrage of bullets immediately followed.

The officers rushed to take cover behind their vehicles, as they returned fire. Parents dashed to grab their children and the elders rushed inside of their home and searched for safety.

Behind the couch, Dillon put another fresh clip inside his 9mm. "Fuck that shit! I ain't going back to prison," he shouted. "I'd rather die first," he continued.

"Courtney Perry! Hey, Courtney Perry, answer me NIGGA!" the Caucasian officer said, but received no answer.

Crawling out from the back of the couch, Dillon saw the mangled bodies of his two dead brothers, lying on the floor. Both had been hit multiple times in the head and chest. Enraged, Dillon grabbed the AK-47 machine gun that was lying next to Perry's hand as he fought back his tears.

Looking at his deceased brothers, Dillon yelled, "You muthafuckas!!! You dirty muthafuckas!!!"

"Come out with your hands in the air! Now," the officer repeated two times. Suddenly, everything was quiet. Police watched as the bullet-riddled front door fell off its hinges. Glass from the shot-up windows covered the porch. "Come out with your hands in the air," the officer repeated.

Running through the front door, holding the loaded AK-47, Dillon fired wildly at the police. As the police returned fire, Dillon was shot in the body, face, and head, inevitably dying in mid-air as he fell. But not before killing two police officers and wounding several more.

A news crew from NBC caught the entire incident live. Watching inside of her hair salon, Summer couldn't believe what she was seeing. As the reporter told the audience the story behind the shootout, Summer couldn't comprehend his words. She couldn't believe that the uncle, whom she had loved, trusted and adored, was the same man responsible for killing her father. Dwight had snatched her *Everything* from her, and now she watched as his three nephews all met a sudden, and horrific end.

Friday Morning
Prince

I had asked Alexander what was up with the hard stare he had given me. He said, "It was nothing," and walked away. After leaving Victor's office, I quickly headed to Summer's salon, where she had been waiting for me.

As I pulled up in front, I noticed her standing outside talking to Latoya. She quickly got into my car and asked me to drive off.

"Where to?" I asked, seeing the stress taking over her beautiful face. "Anywhere, I don't care," she said. "Are you okay? What's wrong?" I said, slowing down on 48th Street. "My Uncle Dwight and his nephews are the reason my father is dead," she said. "The cop!"

"Yeah, he had my father set up. And his nephews were the ones who robbed and killed him," Summer said, as her tears heavily dropped from her eyes. "I'm so sorry, Baby. Don't worry. They'll all get what they deserve," he promised. "They're dead! All of them," Summer said. "What! What happened?"

"Dwight killed himself yesterday inside of his job. And his nephews got killed in a shootout with the police last night. It's all over the news and on the front page of the paper. Everyone's talking about it," she cried. "I'm so sorry, Summer," I said, pulling over to the side of the road and giving her a much-needed hug.

"Everything is so messed up! It's just so crazy! My mother, Aunt Helen, my dad, and now Uncle Dwight! All of them dead! Why is all of this happening to me, Prince? Why?" she cried harder. "You'll always have me, Summer. I'm not going anywhere, baby," I said, hopeful that my words could provide some comfort during this inconsolable time.

"Prince, I love you so much. But I'm so afraid," Summer said, looking into my eyes. "Afraid of what?" I said. "I'm afraid of losing you too. I don't know what I will do if anything ever happened to you, Prince." Her words penetrated me. There was no way I was leaving her life. She was my family, my love, and I had to be the rock she needed now and always.

A Few Hours Later

Inside her bedroom, Keisha had just hung up the phone with her anonymous friend. After taking a shower and getting dressed, she laid back down on the bed and called Summer.

"Hello," Summer answered. "What's up? It's me," Keisha said. "Did you feed Love like I asked you?" "Yeah, I fed her. And cleaned up her shit," Keisha said. "Thanks, Keisha. What's up, girl?" Summer asked.

"Where are you?" Keisha said, taking a sip of Pepsi soda. "I'm chillin out in the park," Summer said. "The park! What are you doing out there?" Keisha asked, being her nosey self. "Prince came to the salon and got me. We just went for a nice long ride, and now we're chillin in the park. I needed a break," Summer admitted.

"Okay, cool. What time will you be back home?" "Around eight. Why what's up?" Summer said, sensing Keisha wanted something. "I need to borrow your car. I have to make a run around nine," Keisha said. "Okay, I'll be home at eight. You can use my car then. Is everything cool?" Summer asked, checking on her friend.

"Everything's fine. I just have to handle some business real quick. I'll be right back. It won't take long," she said. Alright, Keisha. I'll see you in a little while. Bye," Summer said, ending the call and laying back across Prince's lap.

After hanging up the phone, Keisha went downstairs to the kitchen and fixed herself a bowl of Frosted Flakes cereal. Sitting at the kitchen table, she picked up the latest Philadelphia Daily News and started reading about the tragic shootout that took place in West Philly the night before.

The front page of the newspaper said: "SHOOTOUT ON 42ND STREET, with a four-page article inside about the three men who were killed by police, and the two officers who had lost their lives in the line of duty. Even Keisha couldn't believe that this real life soap opera all tied back to Sonny; the deceased father of her unborn child.

~~~

Once all the customers had gotten their hair done, Latoya closed up the shop and went upstairs to her apartment. Earl was sitting on the steps waiting for her, and she was delighted to see him.

"Hey, big boy," Latoya said, giving him a kiss on the lips. "I've been waiting for you," Earl said, grabbing her hands and leading her into his apartment.

Walking through the living room and straight into his bedroom, Earl slung her across his bed. As Latoya sat on the bed getting undressed, Earl stood up and undressed as well. Once they were naked, Earl went into his dresser drawer and took out a condom and a black scarf.

"Lay back on this pillow," he said, taking a seat next to Latoya on the bed. As she followed his instructions, Earl took the black scarf and wrapped it around her eyes. "Don't say a word," he said.

Lying in total darkness, Latoya felt Earl's long warm tongue traveling up and down her body. After placing one of his pillows under Latoya's plush, round, soft ass, he slowly began eating her wet pussy. Latoya's hard moans filled the room with every single lick and twirl. Being blindfolded while Earl devoured her pussy turned her on like never before. The excitement of not seeing and just feeling Earl's tongue added intensity and caused her to soak the pillow.

As the blindfold loosened, Earl tied it back tightly, and then he stretched Latoya's arms out. Latoya was mesmerized in complete darkness, as Earl kissed around her plump erect nipples. After working his way back down to her pussy, he picked back up where he had left off. With his long middle finger inside her ass, he continued to massage Latoya's sensitive clit with his remarkable tongue.

Once again, her hard moans filled the air. "Ooooh, baby, that feels so good!!! Don't stop!!! I'm about to cum," Latoya cried out, as her body began shaking uncontrollably. Turning Earl on with her sexual pleading, Earl sucked on her pussy wildly. "Ooooh, ohhhhhhhhhh, PLEASE BABY PLEASE!!! I'M CUMIN. I'M CUMMING," Latoya said, as a wonderful intense orgasm erupted.

Blindfolded, and trying to get her body to stop trembling, Latoya took a deep few breaths. Earl placed on his extra-large magnum condom. Eating her out was only phase one, and Earl had plenty of rounds in him. Her pussy was about to get beat, and she wasn't going to get any breaks!

North Philly

After parking Summer's Lexus around the corner from Boo's house, Keisha put on her dark Chanel shades and then got out of the car. The street was dark with only one tall street light providing a glimpse of light. Approaching Boo's house, Keisha noticed Boo's silver Range Rover was nowhere in sight.

Inside the small black mailbox was an extra key; Keisha had stashed there. Making sure no one saw her, she used the key to gain entry inside the home. While inside, Keisha broke a back window with a broomstick and then she pulled the window up. Next, she headed upstairs to the empty bedroom. Fifteen minutes later, Keisha walked out of the front door holding a green trash bag in her hands. After making sure the front door was locked, she walked around the corner and got back into the car.

As she drove away, she smiled, tasting sweet revenge on her lips. Looking inside of the bag filled with drug money, Keisha closed it back up and continued to drive to Summer's.

When Keisha was inside of Boo's house, she had ransacked the bedroom making it look like a robbery. She then went to Boo's stash spot, underneath the large dresser, and took every single dollar that was there. In total, she walked away with two hundred and twenty-thousand dollars of Tonyman's money. Payback is a bitch and ain't nothing worse than a woman scorned!

Inside Earl's Apartment

"How do you feel?" Earl asked, laying his sweaty naked body next to Latoya. "I feel like I won't be able to make it to work tomorrow. Does that answer your question?" Latoya said as she massaged his scalp. "You'll be alright," Earl laughed, admiring the indirect compliment.

"Really. I guess you would say that because you ain't got ten thick, strong inches beating your insides up," she said. "Oh, you complaining now?" Earl smiled. "Never that, Big Boy. As long as you bring it, I can take it," she smiled. "Oh, is that right?" Earl asked. "Yes, that's right!"

Turning Latoya onto her stomach, Earl got on top of her sweaty naked body and started fucking her from behind. All it took was for something sassy to come out of Latoya's mouth to make his ten inches rise. The duo was back at it!

CHAPTER 16

Early Saturday Morning

After being out all night partying at Club Flow and Club Evolution, on Delaware Avenue, Boo, Cheeze and their two attractive female friends had breakfast at the IHOP restaurant on City Line Avenue. After breakfast, they went back to Boo's house in North Philly. As Cheeze and one of the lovely females lip-locked on the couch, Boo and the other female walked upstairs into his bedroom. Entering his bedroom, Boo's heart almost fell from his chest as he looked around at the ransacked room. Quickly running over to the dresser where he kept his stash, Boo couldn't believe that he had been robbed. Running down the stairs, Boo was surprised to see Cheeze already fucking his female acquaintance on the couch.

"Cheeze!!! Cheeze!!! Get up man; I've been robbed!!!" Boo shouted, running through the house searching for intruders. Seeing that the back window was broken out and pushed up, Boo raced back into the living room. "Somebody robbed me, man! They got in from the fuckin kitchen window! They got all of Tonyman's money," Boo nervously shouted.

Once Cheeze put his clothes back on, the girls stood around looking confused, as Boo paced the floor.

"Sorry ladies but y'all have to go," Boo said, opening up the front door. "Go where? We live in Jersey," one of the females said. "Here, catch a fuckin cab," Boo shouted, as he went into his pocket and pulled a hundred dollar bill from the wad. After giving the upset females the cash, Boo rushed them out of the front door.

"Man, what the fuck I'ma do? Tonyman wants his money tonight," Boo said, in a scared tone as he took a seat on the couch. "Call him and tell him what happened," Cheeze said. "Man, he ain't tryin to hear that shit! He told me the other day that he needed his money today," Boo snapped.

"Well, what we gonna do?" Cheeze said. "You mean what I'ma do? He don't care about you, Cheeze. I'm the one who gets my shit from him. FUCK! FUCK! FUCK! I wonder who the fuck got me! Somebody's been watching me. Somebody close. I don't show people my moves, so it's gotta be somebody close," Boo rammed. "Who do you think it could be?" Cheeze said.

"I don't know, man. Who knows? It could be anybody. But how the fuck did they know that I wouldn't be home all night?" Boo said.

Hearing the phone ring, Cheeze picked it up and answered. "Hello," he said. "Yeah, one minute," Cheeze said, walking over to Boo holding the phone. "Who is it?" Boo said. "It's Tonyman!" Cheeze said, passing him the phone.

"Tonyman, what's up?" Boo said. "You nigga! What time will you be in the city?" he asked. "Uhm, we have a little problem," Boo nervously said. "Something happened." "And what's that?" Tonyman asked, not in the mood to hear any excuses. "Somebody robbed me for all the money."

"What!!! Nigga, are you trying to play me? Do you think this is a fucking game," Tonyman yelled into the phone.

"Huh, you fuckin stupid ass punk!!! You better get my fuckin money, Boo! And I mean tonight! Not tomorrow. Tonight!!!"

"Tonyman, I'ma need some time," Boo pleaded. "You had time, nigga! More than enough. Now have my money tonight! Or next week I'll be telling ya motha over there in South Philly what a nice kid you were at your funeral!!! And don't try to run, Boo, 'cause I got niggaz where you sleep," Tonyman said, ending the phone call.

Looking at the telephone in his hand, Boo threw it down on the floor. "What the fuck I'ma do? Where can I get two-twenty in the next few hours, Cheeze? Where?" Boo shouted. That was an answer Cheeze didn't have for his right-hand man. For now, the two sat on the couch racking their scattered brains about their next move.

Summer

Last night, after I dropped off my car to Keisha, Prince and I went back to his condo for another delicious night of lovemaking. As he slept, I couldn't help but stare at the four abstract portraits on the walls. I don't know why, but there was something about the one called "Pain" that gave me the creeps. The more I thought about it; I still didn't know what to make of it. And the more I learned about Prince; I knew this picture had to have a profound meaning. Prince didn't just have stuff. Anything he had had a purpose. Prince is an eccentric man, and I've never met a person so adroit in my life. From the way he spoke to the way he made love, everything about him interested and fascinated me.

Looking at him as he slept so peacefully, a smile filled with delight blossomed onto my face. Right then, I knew I loved him more than anything in the world. With Prince, I had played the game of love and stood victorious.

Opening his beautiful brown eyes, he caught me staring at him. "You okay, Baby?" he said, showing me that one of a kind smile of his. "I'm fine. As long as I got you, I'm alright," I said, leaning over and giving him a sweet kiss on his full lips.

Later That Afternoon

"What the fuck I'ma gonna do, Cheeze?" Boo said, driving through Fairmount Park. "Stop worrying, Boo. I said you could stay in my apartment for a while. At least until things settle down," Cheeze said, checking a text message on his phone.

"Well, I'ma still keep my gat on me just in case," Boo said, driving with his 9mm on his lap. "Who the hell could have robbed me?" Boo snapped. "Boo, stop trippin', dawg. Everything will be alright. Just stay at my spot until you figure this shit all the way out. Tonyman probably sent a few of his henchmen by your crib already. So you can't go back there. You'll be safe in West Philly."

"Thanks, Cheeze, but I'm still fucked up about this shit. Something just ain't right, dawg."

As Boo continued to drive through the park, he couldn't help but think about the robbery. He now had a bounty on his head, and the only thing that could get it cleared was for him to come up with the money he owed Tonyman. But, at present, he had no cash. He was a dead man walking.

Brooklyn, New York.

Shakira watched from her bedroom window as Tonyman, and two of his men got inside of his black Lincoln Navigator. After overhearing her brother was on his way to Philadelphia to make an example out of Boo, she waited for Tonyman to leave and then quickly called him.

"Hello," Boo said, answering his cell phone. "Boo, it's me, Shakira," she said. "Shakira, what's up? I'm pretty busy right now," Boo said, trying to get her off the phone quickly. "I called to tell you that my brother is on his way to Philly. He's coming with a few of his stupid ass friends, and they're looking for you. I heard him say something about you owing him money, and how he's not letting that ride. I just want you to be safe because his friends don't do much talking," Shakira said.

"Thanks, Shakira, but I'll be cool. When they get to my house, I won't be there," Boo said arrogantly. "But I heard Tonyman say they won't have no problem finding you," she warned. "Shakira, don't worry about me. I'll be cool." "Well, I can't help it. Besides I have something else to tell you, Papi," she said. "What's that?" Boo said. "I just found out that I'm pregnant," Shakira said. "What!" Boo said, pulling over to the side of the road. "Yeah, I was gonna tell you when you came back to New York. I wanted to surprise you," she said.

"Pregnant! Is it mine?" Boo snapped. "Boo, you're the only person that I slept with without protection. I wouldn't tell you I was pregnant if you weren't the father. And if you need a blood test I'll get that because I don't need to trap you," she said."

"Damn, Shakira! Does Tonyman know?" Boo said as he shook his head in utter disbelief. "No, I haven't told him." "How far are you?" Boo said, scratching his head. "I'm only a few weeks, and please, don't ask me to get rid of it because I'm keeping my baby. I don't do abortions," she said.

"Look, Shakira, we're gonna have to talk about this, but right now I have to find a way to get your brother his money. As soon as I get things right, I'ma call you, and we'll talk," he said. "Okay, just remember, don't go near your house and please watch yourself because my brother has a way of finding whoever he's looking for," she said. "Alright, Shakira. I'll call you soon," he said, feeling overwhelmed with the amount of catastrophic events currently happening in his life. "Bye, bye, Papi," Shakira said before she hung up the phone.

Pulling back onto the road, Boo felt like he had crashed. His world was slowly closing in on him. In less than twenty-four hours, he had gone from being a man with a stash, dispensable cash, endless beautiful women, and hood riches; to a man on the run, with an unwanted child and girl, who couldn't show his face in public because it could be the last time he saw the light of day.

~~~

Inside of her bedroom, Keisha had just finished counting the money from inside of the bag. Sitting on the bed next to Love, Keisha stared hard at the two-hundred and twenty thousand dollars in cash that was on top of the dresser. This was the largest amount of money that her eyes had ever seen. She felt as if she had just won the lottery.

After placing the money back inside of the green plastic bag, she put it in the back of the closet. Keisha thought about Boo and how he was undoubtedly losing his mind behind the missing cash, and the taste of revenge made her smile brightly.

Standing in front of the mirror, Keisha looked at her bruised face. "Nigga, you just don't know how bad you fucked up," Keisha said directly into the mirror. "I told you after that Mark incident you'd never put your fucking hands on me again. Now you'll see I wasn't playing. Fuck you, Boo!"

Keisha gently rubbed her swollen black eye before taking a seat back on the bed.

"This was much bigger than you anyway," Keisha said, as a tear ran down her aching face. "And you don't even know the half," she said, as she lay back on the bed next to Love.

CHAPTER 17

Saturday Night
Summer

After an enjoyable time at Warm Daddy's, Prince and I, along with Latoya and Earl, got into Prince's car and headed to Atlantic City. Atlantic City was like a miniature Vegas on the east coast. It didn't have as many hotels and casinos, but you could go there and walk the boardwalk, win or lose some cash, have some great food and salt water taffy's, and enjoy oneself.

As Prince drove, I sat back and listened to the truth-filled words of Angie Stone, while Latoya and Earl sat in the backseat, unable to keep their hands and lips off of one another. It was good to see Latoya happy for a change. She had gone through so many problems with Nolan's father, Robert, that I thought she would have a nervous breakdown. It seemed as though Earl came into her life at the perfect time.

I knew when Earl had completed his rental application that he would like Latoya once he saw her. I could have moved someone else into the vacant apartment; there were a few other candidates whose credit and background checks were just as good as Earl's, but something told me the two of them would hit it off real good. Seeing that he was single with no kids, I had to play my part and try to hook her up. And I think she knew I had a small part to play in their hookup because every once in a while she'd look me in my eyes, with a big smile on her face and whisper, "Thanks."

Inside the lovely and elegant Taj Mahal Casino and Hotel, Prince and I were at one of the crap tables while Latoya and Earl played the slot machines. After a few hours of gambling, eating and talking, it was almost four in the morning. Prince decided that we should stay the night and nonchalantly paid for everyone's suites.

Inside our suite, the two of us sat nude inside of the bubbling Jacuzzi. With the lights dimmed, and the radio playing some smooth R&B, we fed each other fresh cherries from a chilled glass bowl. After placing both of my arms around Prince's shoulders, I positioned myself and sat on top of him. Feeling his rock hard dick slowly entering me from beneath the water, I closed my eyes and held on.

As the two of us made wonderful music with our bodies, I could feel the intensity of my orgasm as it peaked. Pulling me closer to his chest, our lips met with a long passionate kiss. As our lips remained locked, I continued to grind slowly on Prince's hard dick. Moments later, we climaxed together.

Lying on top of his chest, breathing hard and heavy, he whispered into my ear, "How's my light shining?" I looked into his eyes and whispered back, "As bright as ever, knowing I'll always have you."

Early Sunday Morning

Boo's eyes almost jumped out of their sockets when he saw Tonyman and two of his men standing over him, pointing their guns at his head. "I told you, motherfucka, I got niggaz where you sleep," Tonyman said, patting Cheeze on the back. "Yo, you set me the fuck up," Boo angrily shouted.

"Business is business, Boo. Ain't that what you always told me? There ain't no love in this game. And best friends become strangers overnight for the right price," Cheeze said proudly. "Nigga, I gave you everything!" Boo shouted. "Everything except your crown! And now I got it," Cheeze said, walking out of the room.

"Fuck you, nigga!" Boo yelled. "No, fuck you, muthafucka!!!" Tonyman said, pulling the trigger and shooting Boo straight through the eye. Tonyman shot Boo two more times in the head, ensuring that he was dead.

"That's for my sister. Now clean this piece of shit up," Tonyman told his men, as he walked out of the room.

After wrapping Boo's corpse in a thick wool blanket, the two men carried it outside and placed it in the back of the Navigator. As Tonyman was about to pull off, Cheeze approached him, and he rolled down the passenger side window.

"So we still have a deal?" Cheeze asked. "What did I tell you, Cheeze? Don't worry; you're the man now. I gave you the other number to call me on. Just do that. But I hope you don't make the same mistake because there won't be no sympathy for you either," Tonyman said. "I won't," Cheeze said, shaking Tonyman's hand and watching as the SUV slowly pulled off.

At no time had Boo recognized that his good friend and right-hand man, Cheeze, was eyeing his spot. Cheeze had grown tired of being second in command, and he wanted to deal with the connect firsthand. So he didn't hesitate to call Tonyman while Boo slept peacefully at his apartment. Cheeze had no remorse in his heart as he placed the deadly call that led to Boo's demise. He allowed greed to lead to his actions as his heart hungered for money, power, and respect.

Returning to his apartment, Cheeze sat down on his couch and grinned. "Business is business," he said to himself, as he picked up his phone and placed a call.

"Hello," a voice said on the other end. "The rabbit has been caught," Cheeze said. "Now I'm the Muthafuckin' Man," he smiled, as he sat back on the sofa feeling worthy of his new promotion.

CHAPTER 18

Sunday Afternoon
Summer

After our Atlantic City getaway, we all decided to come back to my house for a little pool party out back. Since I never opened the shop on Sundays today was a great day to enjoy the pool.

On the way back from A.C., we stopped by Latoya's so she and Earl could grab their swim gear. Prince already had some shorts at my house. In fact, he had his own drawer in my bedroom, so we didn't have to pass his house to pick anything up.

As Prince pulled up into the driveway, I was surprised to see Keisha standing out front. She had a pair of dark shades on her face and two suitcases beside her. She smiled when we pulled up.

Prince and Earl headed inside the house. Latoya and I stayed outside with Keisha.

"Where are you going?" I curiously asked looking down at her suitcases. "I'm leaving, Summer. Thanks for everything," Keisha said. "Where are you going?" Latoya asked. Suddenly a brand new Acura turned the corner and pulled up in front of Summer's townhouse.

"I'm going with him," Keisha said, as her smile grew bright. Seeing Cheeze behind the wheel, Latoya or I could not believe our eyes. "So that's the other person you were talking about?" Latoya said. "What other person?" I questioned. "What are y'all two talking about?" I asked getting frustrated that I was out of the loop. "It's a long story, but Latoya will fill you in," Keisha said. "Keisha, you just can't start messing around with Boo's friend. You're just asking for more trouble, "I said, in a sincere tone.

"Summer, Boo won't be around to cause any more trouble," Keisha said abruptly. And I left that statement alone. I knew enough about the streets when it was time to be quiet. Moving on, I thought to myself.

"Keisha, will you be alright? It ain't cool to leave one situation and go back to the same kind. Don't you think it's too soon?" I asked, concerned about her mental and physical wellbeing.

"Summer, I love you girl, but you can't live my life. And you either, Latoya. Cheeze and I will be fine. He's nothing like Boo, and he already knows that I'm pregnant by someone else. But trust, he doesn't care because he cares about me. And you know how I am when I want what I want. Unlike y'all two, the regular nine-to-five type of guy can't satisfy me. All I'll do is use them. I need excitement in my life, and you two should know that already. Look, just continue to be there for me. That's all I want," Keisha said, as the three of us shared a warm group hug.

"I'll be back at work in a few weeks, but right now I wanna get away for a while, so I can go clear my head. So much has happened in the past weeks, and I need to recover. I just need some time," Keisha said sadly, as we hugged once more.

Latoya and I grabbed one of the suitcases and walked her over to the car. Opening the back door, we put the luggage in the back seat and Keisha got in the front passenger seat.

"Take care of my girl, Cheeze," I said, leaning into the window. "Don't worry, Summer, she'll be okay," Cheeze assured me.

Backing away from the car, Latoya and I watched as Cheeze and Keisha pulled off. "I love y'all," Keisha yelled out of the window. "We love you," Latoya, and I said, as the car headed down the street.

~~~

"Here you go, baby," Keisha said, passing the large bag of money she had taken out of the suitcase to Cheeze. "Did you take the twenty-five," he said. "Yeah, I got it. Thanks," Keisha said, leaning over and giving Cheeze a kiss.

"How does your eye feel?" Cheeze asked. "It feels better," Keisha said to her new Boo. "You're still beautiful. That eye will heal soon enough, and we don't need to revisit the past. That shit is over," Cheeze said, as the new couple drove on.

Summer

Seated in comfortable beach chairs, Prince and I watched as Latoya and Earl played in the pool. As the hot scorching sun beamed down on us, the music from the radio played some R&B goodies. Listening to Anita Baker's, Caught Up in the Rapture of Love, I could relate to every single word the vocalist was singing.

Sipping on strawberry Daiquiri, I looked over at Prince, as he stood up from his beach chair. He walked over to me, and he reached down and picked me up into his strong arms. Knowing I was about to be plunged into the water, I squeezed the tip of my nose with my fingers, as he jumped into the pool. For the rest of the afternoon, we all enjoyed the hot sun, the smooth, soulful music, and the cool water.

As the sun began to set, we dried ourselves off and got dressed. Then Prince and I dropped Latoya and Earl off at home. On our way back to my house, I couldn't wait to be wrapped in Prince's sturdy arms. All I felt when I looked at him was love. He was all I needed!

~~~

After burying Boo's corpse somewhere deep inside the vast New Jersey woods, Tonyman, and his two men returned to Brooklyn. Entering his huge home, he immediately yelled out for Shakira. After getting no response, he frustratingly walked upstairs into her bedroom. Opening the door, he realized that she had left while he was in Philly. Seeing the white piece of paper laying on top of her made-up bed, Tonyman picked up the letter and began reading it.

Dear Tonyman,

I left because I know you'll soon find out the truth about me and Boo being together. I never meant to go behind your back, but there was something I saw in Boo that I never saw in any other man. You told me over and over about watching the people I chose to be with, and I did try to be cautious and pick the best person for me. He's into me and I dig him a lot.

And I understand why you are so overprotective when it came to me, but sometimes you are too overprotective. I love you so much, but you have to let me make my mistakes and live my life. I would never do anything to put you in danger, Tonyman. I have your back. You're all that I ever really had. You raised me while our parents stayed in Columbia, and I love you deeply for that. I love you for helping me become a woman. But you have to let go now.

If you don't know by now, I'm pregnant with Boo's child. And I pray that you didn't do anything stupid to my child's father. I left because I know once you found out you would be mad at me and try to make me get rid of my baby. I know you! That's why I left the house and took some money to hold me over for a while. I will call you from time to time, but I will not return home until I have my child. And hopefully with your blessing, you'll let me and Boo be together.

Love Always, Your One & Only Sister,
Shakira

Sitting down on the edge of the bed, Tonyman held his head down. Not only did his baby sister run away from home, but he had just murdered and buried the corpse of her unborn child's father.

After numerous attempts of trying to reach Shakira on her cell phone, he was unable to get in touch with her. Sitting back on the bed, Tonyman thought about how one day he may have to look his niece or nephew in the face, knowing that he was the one responsible for their father's absence. Walking out of Shakira's bedroom and down the hall to his room, Tonyman couldn't believe that his baby sister was gone. He would have to find her and force her to get an abortion. The hunt was on, and the clock was ticking.

Later That Night

"Baby, what's wrong?" Prince said as Summer lay in his arms crying. "I miss my dad, Prince! I just really miss my daddy so much that my heart feels like it's breaking."
"I know you do, Baby. I know you do," Prince said comforting her. "It just doesn't seem right without him being here. I still can't believe all that has happened. My father, my uncle. I...I...just can't believe it," she cried.

"Everything happens for a reason, Summer. God picks and chooses, and we shouldn't question His decisions. It hurts to admit it, but we have no control over when we go. We are here for a limited time and then we are off to what's next for us. The time you shared with your father was priceless. And I wish I could give you guys more time because I hate seeing you hurting the way you do. But, I can't. The best thing we can do is try to adjust to things as best as we can, and strengthen our bond. We have to be strong for one another. And I remember you saying how much your father wanted to be back with your mother. How lately he had been saying that often, too often for your comfort. He could have been preparing you for things because he felt something. We just never know," Prince said, holding her tight in his arms.

"I know. I just miss hearing his voice or seeing him laugh and making jokes in the barbershop with all his friends. I really wish I could see him get mad at Leroy, then smile and give him twenty dollars one more time," Summer said, as she reminisced. "Well, he will always live in you," Prince said, rubbing his hand over her heart.

"I know, and I'll make sure of that. But I wish I could have one more day," Summer said, as her pain filled tears dripped from her eyes.

CHAPTER 19

Montego Bay, Jamaica
Two Weeks Later
Prince

Walking down the gorgeous beach holding hands, Summer and I sat down in a comfortable spot a few feet away from our beach house villa. I waited to bring her back to Jamaica for this special occasion.

"What's wrong with you today? You haven't been yourself?" she said. "Look out at the sun," I said, pointing out at the ocean. "It's beautiful, isn't it?" Summer smiled

"Yes, it's very beautiful. But see, its beauty only lasts for a while, then it goes away. And when the moon comes out to replace it, it too only lasts a while until the sun returns."

"What are you saying, Prince? I'm confused," Summer said, looking into my eyes. "I'm saying that even though the sun and moon are extremely beautiful to look at and appreciate, they don't last forever. Only one thing lasts forever."

"And what's that?" Summer asked. "Love. True love never comes and goes, and that's what I feel when I'm with you, Summer," I said, reaching into my white linen shorts and pulling out the three-caret platinum engagement ring.

"Will you be my wife?" I said, looking into her watery brown eyes. "Summer, will you marry me?" I said, now on bended knee.

As she cried tears that I had hoped were filled with excitement, Summer remained frozen and speechless. Nervously shaking, she tearfully said, "Yes, Yes, Yes! Prince,

I'll marry you," as she fell to her knees in front of me. After sliding the ring on her finger, we shared a kiss that solidified our strong love that we wanted to be permanent.

Later that night, inside of our private beach house, we made fiery fanatical love. We had found our happiness in each other. Something we both craved and desired. All of my life I had searched for a special woman who would help me turn my life around. Through the long process of soul searching, I had only hurt myself by allowing lust to lead my choices. That was until I met Summer. The woman who would ultimately become my bride.

They say everything happens for a reason. And she's my reason! My reason to be the best husband that I can be, while at the same time being her best friend and soul mate. For the first time in a very long time in my life, I was happy. This feeling touched the depths of my once crying soul and healed me. A feeling that I prayed would last a lifetime as I journeyed on my path, hand in hand, heart to heart, with my future wife, Summer.

Summer's Hair Salon

The last customer had just left the shop. Latoya and the newly hired assistant, Katrina, were inside cleaning up while Keisha waited by the door for Cheeze to pick her up. While Summer was away in Jamaica, Latoya and Keisha had been running the shop in her absence.

For the past few weeks, Keisha and Cheeze had been together. Cheeze had moved out of his small West Philly apartment, and he and Keisha moved into a much larger and more expensive place in Center City. Keisha enjoyed the excitement that came with being with her new man. Cheeze was a street dude. One who wasn't afraid of the game he played and he liked to play dirty. After taking over Boo's empire, his street status blew up making his girl, Keisha, admire him even more.

Cheeze pulled up in front of the shop in his brand new champagne colored SL500 Mercedes Benz that sat on 22" chrome rims. Keisha walked over to Latoya and said, "Cheeze is here. I'll call you tonight." She then gave Latoya a warm hug and kiss on the cheek. "Alright, don't forget to call me. I know you will," Latoya said, as she continued sweeping the hair off the floor.

As Keisha walked out of the door, a midnight black tinted Chevy Impala pulled up beside Cheeze's Mercedes. Leaning out of the passenger window, holding two loaded 9mm's in his hand, a man wearing a black ski mask began unloading his clips into Cheeze's car; hitting Cheeze in his back and chest. Cheeze was struck, but still able to grab his gun from underneath his seat and fire off a few rounds himself.

The car sped off quickly down the street, as Cheeze opened his door and continued to fire his gun at the moving vehicle. Holding his chest, he limped over to the sidewalk. Keisha was laid out on the ground motionless. Cheeze fell to his knees before he could reach her as his blood continued to swiftly exit his body. He struggled to breathe, slumping hard to the ground.

Racing out of the salon, Latoya saw Keisha and Cheeze, lying a few feet away from one another, bleeding out. A loud scream sprinted from her soul as she ran to Keisha's side.

"No!!! No!!!" Latoya screamed, seeing that a bullet had entered Keisha's chest. Holding her friend in her arms, Latoya continued to scream and call out to God. She pleaded with God to save her friend, but there would be no mercy. Tonight no favors would be granted because a debt had to be paid.

On this hot summer night, Cheeze and Keisha's bodies lay dead on the sidewalk, along with Keisha and Sonny's unborn child. The fast life that Keisha loved being a part of came with many consequences. It was a life that glitters but only has momentary shine. Not too many people made it out alive, and it's easy to get caught up quickly in this life. Tonight her love for this life had brought deadly consequences, and she paid the ultimate penalty.

Frackville Prison

Malcolm waited for someone to pick up the phone. Hearing the prison voice message, the man quickly accepted the call.

"Hello," a man's voice said. "Yo, what's up?" Malcolm said. "Y'all handle that?" he asked. "Everything is taken care of. Boo is smiling in his grave for sure," the man said. "Thanks, dawg. I'll holla at you," Malcolm said, hanging up the phone with a sense of satisfaction.

After going back into his cell, Malcolm sat down on his hard cot and finished looking at the pictures of his cousin Boo. "I told you I'd get them," he said to himself. "I told you."

While Malcolm sat in prison, he had found out that Cheeze and Keisha were a couple. Everyone was talking about how Boo had suddenly disappeared and Cheeze was now running his drug turf, driving new cars, and fucking his woman. Malcolm didn't have to put two and two together. It was obvious that they had set his cousin up. Through his street connects, Malcolm put a hit out on both their heads. And tonight it was paid off. Business is business.

One Week Later

Leaving Keisha's burial, Summer, Latoya, Nolan, and Earl were inside the long black limo. After Sonny's funeral, Prince couldn't take another one, so he decided to stay home. Summer understood. She never liked funerals much herself, but today she had to be there to see her best friend leave this world and enter another one.

Wrapped in Latoya's arms, Summer couldn't believe that Keisha was gone. Her family lineage had grown shorter; having never had a chance to meet her new sister or brother. The grief that Summer felt was overwhelming, and it sickened her.

As the black limousine pulled up in front of Prince's condo, Summer saw him standing out front. Seeing Prince waiting for her, Summer gave everyone a hug and kiss, and then she exited the limo.

"I'm sorry, baby," Prince said, holding his crying woman inside of his arms. "I'm so, so sorry that you had to go through this again," Prince said.

As Summer continued to cry, she remained speechless inside of Prince's arms. Once the limo drove down the street, Summer and Prince went inside.

"I love you, Prince," Summer finally spoke. "I love you so much and every day I thank God for bringing you into my life. Don't leave me," Summer cried!

One Week Later
Northeast Philly
Prince

Inside Victor's office, I sat on the couch staring at the photo he had just given me. This was the last man I had to kill for Victor and Alexander, and I was looking forward to getting this last kill done and over with. The man's name was Boris Novikov, and I could sense that both Victor and Alexander had really wanted this man disposed of. I noticed that neither could look at the photo without scrunching with anger. Since I had known Victor, I've never seen him this way about any of the men that he wanted dead. I knew that whoever this man was, he had done something so treacherous that both these brothers still harbored the hatred to this day. And looking in their eyes, I could tell they wanted their personal pains to come to an end with his death.

"Where and when?" I asked. "Miami. South Beach," Victor said. "But you must leave tonight, Prince. I'll make sure everything is ready for you," Alexander said, walking towards the door. "Make that for two," I said, watching Alexander stop in his tracks.

"For two? Who are you taking?" Victor asked. "I'm taking my fiancé. Don't worry she won't know what's going on. I'll tell her that I have some meetings to attend. She'll understand," I said. "I think that will be too risky," Victor warned. "We'll be okay. We will be just another couple enjoying the city."

After speaking in their native Russian language, Victor finally agreed. "Okay Prince, you can take her along, but please my good friend, don't mess this up," Victor said, in a serious voice. "This is very important," Alexander added. "Very, very important, Victor added. "I know. I can tell," I said, shaking their hands before walking out of the office.

As I got inside my car, Victor and Alexander stood in the doorway watching me as I pulled off. I can't explain it, but something didn't feel right with them. Something was wrong. I could sense it in my bones. But I also felt like I was paranoid because I was at the end of my hit list. I told myself to focus on my future. That I was finally moving my life in the direction, I always wanted.

Holding the photo in my hand, I couldn't help but stare at it once more. Killing this man was the key to my freedom. After him, there would be no more. My debt would be paid.

As I drove down the street, my eyes watered. Seeing Summer's face in each teardrop, and thinking of my future life with her; I had to get this hit done and over with as quickly as I could.

CHAPTER 20

South Beach, Miami
Prince

The Delano was the classiest hotel on South Beach. Quiet and exquisite, with a gleaming poolside bar just a few steps away from the private beach; it was filled with beautiful white curtains, dim candles, and crisp tablecloths all throughout. This was where all the Hollywood stars stayed from Will and Jada to Ashton and Demi. On any given day, you could see one of Hollywood's A-list celebrities walking through the halls.

After Summer and I unpacked, we took a shower and got dressed. We then rented a black Ford Expedition to get us around town. I had already known much about Miami from the many trips I had taken there when I wanted to enjoy the warm weather and scenery. I figured I could find a good spot that Summer and I could enjoy.

Tonight my love and I had a wonderful lobster meal at the Tantra Restaurant, on Pennsylvania Avenue. Afterward, we were lucky enough to get into the exclusive "Mynt" Club. Fortunately, I knew the doorman from one of my previous trips. He turned out to be an art lover and my appreciation for paintings scored me some bonus points, and I was told I'd always be treated like VIP. Tonight he held true to his words.

The Mynt Club was located on Collins Avenue, and it was one of South Beach's best clubs. The long, narrow club is a vision in glossy green, with earth-toned couches and equally toned patrons sidling up to the bar. I knew Summer needed a break from all of the drama she had endured back in Philly, and this seemed to be the spot to lighten her load. Seeing her smile, laugh, dance, and drink, brought comfort to my soul. Soon I'd have the pen to my storybook, and the two of us could fill our days with whatever stories and memories we decided to create.

Philadelphia, PA

After dropping Nolan off at his grandmother's, Latoya and Earl went back to his apartment. As Earl lay back on the bed naked, Latoya climbed on top of the bed to join him. "I think I'm ready now," Latoya said, grabbing Earl's massive ten-inch dick in her hands.

Lying back, Earl felt Latoya's warm lips on the tip of his dick. She then placed it inside her wet, warm mouth and started sucking him off. Up and down she went, twirling her tongue, and sucking his massive python like a natural pro; while massaging his balls at the same time. The wonderful feeling sent Earl to cloud-nine and beyond. Now it was he who moaned and squirmed with every touch.

Feeling himself about to cum, he reached and grabbed the top of Latoya's bouncing head. "I'm about to CUM!!!" Earl said, as his long thin legs began shaking. "I'm about to CUM!!!" he cried out, again.

His warnings didn't slow down the professional. Latoya was an expert, and she knew you weren't supposed to talk with your mouth full.

Earl could no longer hold it as Latoya deep throated him and slightly gagged, turning him on even more; so he exploded deeply into her welcoming throat. Latoya didn't budge and kept his dick inside of her mouth as Earl begged her to take it out. The sensitivity caused him to tremble, and he repeated, "I can't take no more. I can't take no more," until she opened up her mouth and slowly allowed him to pull out. His tip was dry because Latoya had swallowed every single drop of his cum and left no traces within sight.

As Earl tried to relax and regain his composure, Latoya climbed on top of him and said "Now it's my turn to take a ride," as she mounted him and went to work.

Prince

Four days passed and I had been watching Boris' every move. Though he was staying at another hotel, The Raleigh, was only a few blocks away from the Delano. Every morning I left my suite while Summer slept peacefully in bed. Each day I'd observe Boris and his two bodyguards. In the morning, they'd take an early morning walk or slight jog around Collins Park. I had observed him midday and in the evening. Now I had found a window of opportunity, and it was just a matter of time.

One night after Summer and I returned to our hotel from a night of partying at the Mansion Club; I was in total shock to see Alexander standing in the lobby.

"Prince, what's going on, my friend?" he said, approaching Summer and me, shaking my hand. "Alexander, what are you doing down here?" I asked. "Just came down to check out beautiful Miami," he smiled. "So this must be your beautiful fiancé," Alexander said. "Yes, this is Summer, the woman I told you about," I said, trying to hide my frustration at his presence. "She's more beautiful than you told me," Alexander smiled, making Summer blush.

"Hello. Prince, where do you know each other from?" Summer asked. "Oh, we work together back in Philadelphia,"

Alexander interrupted. "Oh, you buy property too," Summer said. "Yes, exactly," Alexander lied. "Are you staying here?" Prince asked. "Yes, I just got myself a room on the fourth floor," Alexander said. "What a coincidence. We're staying on the fourth floor too," Summer said.

"Summer, can you please give me and Alexander a minute? I need to talk to him about some work related issues. It's good that he's here because it was on my mind heavy and now is a good time to straighten things out," Prince said. "Sure, baby. Take your time. I'm going to the room," Summer said, sensing that something was wrong. "Bye, Alexander," she said waving to Alexander and walking away.

"What the fuck are you doing down here, man?" I angrily stated once Summer was out of sight. "If Boris or any of his men see you, you'll fuck everything up," I snapped. "Don't worry, Prince, he won't see me. I know where he's staying. And don't worry, I know how to stay out of the way," Alexander said.

"What the fuck is going on, Alexander? You never came before, why now?" I asked. "Because, Prince, this is very important! There can be no mistakes with Boris," Alexander whispered. "Did I ever make a mistake before? Why would I start now? What else is going on, Alexander? Why did Victor send you?" Prince frustratingly asked.

"Prince, calm down, my friend, and stop worrying yourself over nothing. I'm here to make sure everything goes right," he said. "Fuck that. I don't like this shit! I'ma call Victor and see what's going on."

"Prince, stop jumping to conclusions, my friend. Victor knows I'm here already," he said. "What's all of this friend crap? You never liked me, and you know it! I know you're jealous of me and your brother's relationship. So save that bullshit," I said, finally telling him exactly what I had noticed. "Why would I be jealous of you and Victor? He's my brother; you're just a friend," he said condescendingly.

"I don't know why, ask yourself. I've asked myself and still haven't come up with a good reason," I fumed. "Prince, you've been drinking a little. You don't know what you're saying," Alexander said. "I don't drink! And I know exactly what I'm saying. I'm telling you, Alexander, just stay out of my way. I work alone, and I won't let you fuck that up now," I said, as I walked away and left Alexander standing in a stupor.

As I walked into my room, seeing Summer's beautiful naked body on top of the bedcovers instantly calmed my frustration.

"Are you okay baby?" she said, in a sweet sexy tone. "I'm fine," I said, taking off my clothes and quickly joining her in bed. "Maybe, tomorrow we can take your friend out to lunch," Summer said. "Maybe, but he just told me he has a lot of running around to do while he's down here. So don't count on it," I said, turning off the lamp by our bed.

"You don't seem like you, baby. Are you sure you're okay?" she asked. "I'm fine. Now come here and let me taste those warm lips of yours," I said, grabbing Summer in my arms.

As we kissed, I couldn't help but think about Alexander and the real reason he was in South Beach. I tried to pretend that everything was okay, but it wasn't. And I knew that Summer could feel something was bothering me. She knew me better than anyone else. Just like I could tell when something was troubling her; we were connected that way.

Alexander was up to something, but exactly what, that's what I needed to know. Hopefully, I would find out soon because I didn't need anything standing in the way of my last hit.

CHAPTER 21

Early The Next Morning

"Hello," Victor said, answering the phone inside of his office.

"Victor, it's me, Prince."

"Prince, how's everything going in Miami?"

"Everything is going fine. But tell me, why did you send Alexander down here?"

"Prince, I knew you would be calling me about that. It's nothing, my friend."

"Then why did you send him? You never did that before. You know I work alone! Why change things now?"

"Prince, please, will you calm down! Alexander was sent down to make sure everything goes good. This particular person is more important to me than all the others!"

"All will go as planned if you just let me do my job, Victor! I don't like this shit at all!"

"Relax my friend. Alexander won't interfere. He's simply down there to make sure things go smoothly. Boris is unlike all the others. He's well protected."

"I know. I've been watching him for five days now."

"Just don't worry about Alexander, my friend. Like I said, Prince, he's only down there to make sure that nothing goes wrong."

"What if Boris or one of his men see him?"

"They won't. Alexander will stay out of the way. He knows how important this is."

"Remember, Victor; this is the last one. No more! No matter what or how much you offer, this is it! I'm finished!"

"I gave you my word, didn't I? So don't you worry. This is the last, Prince. Just get it done."

"Don't worry about that. It will get done, today."

"You make sure you call me as soon as the job is done. Do you remember the code I gave you, Prince?"

"Yeah, Moscow," I remembered. "As soon as it's done, I'll call you."

"Please don't forget, as soon as it's done and not a minute later."

"I told you I'll call you! Why is that so important all of a sudden? Why can't you wait till I get back and show you the photos like always?"

"Because this time is different. This time, my friend, I need to know as soon as it's all over."

"Alright, Victor, whatever you want," Prince said, ending the call.

Philly

That afternoon, after Latoya, and her son Nolan, had finished walking Love around the neighborhood, Nolan and Latoya sat out in front of the house talking.

"Mommy, why did those bad men kill Aunt Keisha?" he asked. "Why did you ask me that, Nolan?" Latoya said shocked. "Because I wanna know why they did it," Nolan said sadly. "Because they were evil. Only evil people do stuff like that," his mother stated.

"Did Aunt Keisha do anything to them?" the curious boy asked. "No...no, she didn't," his mother said, becoming irritated as that day played over in her mind. "Then why does God let evil people do stuff like that?"

"God doesn't let them. They do it on their own, Nolan. God doesn't have anything to do with evilness," she said to him. "But every day people get shot, and people die. Why does God let that happen?" he continued. "I told you, Nolan, that isn't because of God's doings. That's all the Devil's work."

"Why doesn't God just kill the Devil then?" he asked. "One day he will," Latoya promised her son. "Then no one else will get shot like Aunt Keisha and Uncle Sonny?" he said, waiting to hear his mother's response. "That's right. Then no one else will get shot again," Latoya said, as her eyes watered up.

"Well, I can't wait till he comes because I don't like when people die all the time," her son said, as his eyes became teary as well. "Don't worry, baby, he'll be here soon," Latoya said, grabbing Nolan in her arms and hugging him tightly. "I love you, Mommy," her loving son said. "I love you too, baby," she cried. "I love you too."

Summer

When I opened my eyes, the first thing I noticed was a white card with a single red rose on top of it. Grabbing it off of the nightstand, I smelled the full beautiful rose and opened up the card. "How's my light shining," the card said. Prince knew what to do and say to get an instant smile on my face; I thought as I put the note back on the nightstand. As I sat in bed, I couldn't wait for Prince to return from his early morning run so I could tell him, "As bright as ever knowing that I'll always have you."

Later That Evening
Prince

I cautiously watched as Boris and two of his men walked inside of the "Casa Tua" Restaurant on James Avenue. All day long I had tailed closely behind the all-white tinted limousine that drove my target around town.

After watching Boris and his bodyguards for five long days and nights, I had enough information to make my move soon. Though his two bodyguards hardly ever left the old man's side, I knew sooner or later Boris would make a mistake just like all of the others.

The Delano

"How are you doing?" Summer said, seeing Alexander inside the hallway. "Not too good," Alexander said, holding his lower back. "Are you okay? Do you need me to call someone?" Summer asked. "No, no, I'm fine. It's just my back has been killing me, that's all. Sometimes it goes out on me. But I'll be okay. Thank you," Alexander said, as he continued to hold his back. "And besides, I'm just a few doors down the hall. I'll be fine," he continued.

"Alright, but if you need me, just knock on the door," Summer said, extending some help to her man's friend. "Oh, I'll be alright. Thanks again," Alexander said. "Bye, now," Summer said, walking into her room holding a large gift bag in her hand.

Philadelphia

While Nolan was in bed asleep, Latoya and Earl were embraced in each other's arms inside the pool. Latoya took Summer up on her offer to stay in her house while she vacationed in Miami. Besides, Summer needed someone to care for Love, and Latoya was good with her lovable puppy.

Tonight Latoya had invited Earl over for a late night swim. After taking off her bathing suit, Latoya threw it on the side of the pool. Seeing the nude beauty, Earl took off his shorts and threw them beside her bathing suit. As the full moon shined down on these two lovers, they began making obsessive love inside the swimming pool.

Latoya rode Earl's thick package like a female rodeo star. The water splashed with each stroke while her hard moans filled the air. "Oooohhhhhhhhh, baby, it feels so good," Latoya yelled out. Turning his love toy around, Earl entered her pussy from behind, and once again Latoya moaned out, and now her legs trembled.

"Ahhh, Earl...Earl, I'm about to CUM AGAIN, AGAIN...DON'T...PLEASE...DON'T STOP...AAHHHH," she yelled, as they continued to enjoy their evening out in the pool.

~~~

Walking out from the Casa Tua Restaurant, Boris, and his two bodyguards stood out front of the entrance. After one of the men whistled for the limousine driver, he immediately put the limo in reverse and backed up for Boris and his two bodyguards. After all three were inside the limo, Boris said to the limo driver, "Take me back to the hotel."

The three men waited for the limo to pull off, but then the tinted window partition rolled down as the doors locked. Holding his loaded 9mm with the attached silencer, Prince fired his weapon precisely at the men. Before any of them could run, scream, or beg for mercy, death had already come and gone.

In the seat next to Prince, the limo driver lay dead from a single bullet to the head. After taking a photo with his small digital camera, Prince rolled the partition back up and pulled off. After driving the limousine to a deserted area, he doused the vehicle with gasoline. Lightening the limo on fire, he walked away as the inferno burned viciously.

Prince walked on the road looking for a ride back to his car; he was able to get a cab. Once he was inside of his SUV, Prince called Victor on his cell phone.

"Hello," Victor answered. "Moscow," Prince said, ending the call and pulling off down Collins Avenue.

The Delano

After hanging up the telephone with Victor, Alexander told the naked young female that she needed to leave quickly. Once dressed, she gladly snatched the money from the table and left the room. It was the fastest two-hundred dollars she had ever made; she thought to herself as she walked down the hallway.

Once Alexander had his clothes on, he walked out of his room and down the hall. Hearing a knock at the door, Summer asked who it was and then opened it once she realized it was her man's male acquaintance.

"Can you please help me lift my luggage from off of the shelf? It's a little bit heavy, and my back is still killing me very badly?" Alexander asked, holding his lower back as if he was in severe pain. "Sure, one minute," Summer said, grabbing her room key off of the table and walking out the door.

"Are you sure you don't want to be seen by a doctor?" "No, really, I'm fine. I'll be okay. I just need to get my luggage," he said. "Did you take any pain medicine for your back?" Summer asked, concerned after seeing how much pain he seemed to be in. "Yeah, I took some aspirin. Didn't help much," Alexander said, as they walked down to his room.

"You're gonna need something much stronger than aspirin for your back. It looks like a muscle relaxer might help," she said. "I'll be okay. It comes and goes," Alexander said, opening up his door.

After they were inside Alexander's room, he quickly shut the door.

CHAPTER 22

Prince

Wiping the tears from my eyes, I still couldn't believe that my nightmare had finally come to an end. Victor and I were done and nothing felt better. All I wanted to do now was marry my Summer and move on with my life.

Driving back to the hotel, my cell phone started ringing.

"Hello," I answered.

"It's me, Alexander."

"What's up, man?"

"Can you come by my room? I have something for you.

"What is it, Alexander?"

"Just come. It's a present from Victor," Alexander said, hanging up the phone.

Pulling into the parking lot, I got out of the SUV and hurried upstairs. Going into my room first, I noticed that Summer wasn't there. I then rushed down the hall to Alexander's room and knocked on the door. After getting no response, I turned the doorknob and walked inside.

"Alexander," I yelled. "I'm in the bedroom," he said. "Come on back."

Walking into the bedroom, my heart suddenly stopped beating. Alexander had Summer wrapped in his arms with a loaded 9mm pointed at her head.

"Prince," Summer tearfully cried. "Let her go, Alexander! You want me, not her," I screamed. "Shut the fuck up! You're not calling the shots here. Now put down your gun. I know you have it on you," Alexander yelled.

"Prince, what's going on?" Summer begged, as her face filled with anxiety and uncertainty. "Put down your gun, Prince, or this bitch will die," Alexander said. Removing my gun from under my t-shirt, I laid it on the floor.

"You happy now? Just let her go, Alexander," I pleaded. "Now put both of your arms up," Alexander demanded of me. "Let her go, Alexander, you got me! Please, don't hurt her!" I begged. "Shut the fuck up and put up your arms like I said!"

Slowly putting my arms in the air, I winked my eye at Summer. "Pain," I said. The word jogged her memory as she remembered the night we talked about the portrait on my wall. She remembered the move that I showed her. And tonight I needed her to do precisely what I had taught her if she wanted to make it out of this room alive.

Summer quickly reversed Alexander's hold, giving me enough time to run over to him and knock him down to the floor. As we fought hard over the gun that fell from Alexander's hand, Summer ran and picked up my gun from the floor.

"Let him go," she said, nervously pointing the gun at Alexander's head. "I said let him go!" Summer yelled.

As we got up from the floor, I picked up Alexander's gun. Without hesitation, I pointed the gun at him and fired three shots into his chest. Falling to the floor, Alexander was dead. Summer stood frozen. She could not comprehend what had just occurred.

"Prince, what's going on?" Summer cried out. "Please, tell me what's going on? Who are you?" she asked. I couldn't speak. So I didn't, as I went around the room wiping off everything that Summer and I had touched.

"I'll tell you later. Give me the gun," I finally said, taking the weapon from Summer's trembling hands. "Just go back to the room. I'll tell you everything later. Please just go," I asked her, as she rushed back to our room.

On the late flight back to Philly, it was my time to tell my truth as we sat in first-class without any passengers immediately around us. I told Summer everything. All about how I met Victor in federal prison. And even about all the men that I had been killing for him. I told her about the fast life I had lived on the streets of Philadelphia, about losing my mother to cancer, and the impact having no knowledge of my father had on me. But most importantly, I told her that every time I had killed a man that a part of me died. I wanted her to understand that I was not a monster. I had done what some would call demonic and unforgivable, but I was not without a soul. I had a debt to pay, and I had done my job.

"If you can't handle this, Summer, I understand. And I won't stop you if you choose to go on without me. I don't even feel as if I have the right to ask you to consider having me as a part of your life. I know what I shared was more than you expected to hear. I am sorry for putting you in danger, and I don't know what else to say...but I love you. And I understand any decisions you need to make for you."

Looking into my eyes Summer said, "I can't live my life without you." "Why not?" I asked surprised that she still wanted to speak to me after what I had put her through. "Because my heart won't let me love anyone else. And there's no one else I'd rather love," she said, reaching over and giving me a firm hug.

For the rest of the flight, we stayed embraced in each other's arms. I knew that Summer was still confused and uneasy about everything, but I also knew that she would forgive me.

I then closed my eyes and said a private prayer to God. Through all of my sins I had always asked for forgiveness. Only God knew the deepness of my heart, and I know it was his judgment that would matter most.

Later that night when we arrived back in Philly, Summer and I went back to my condo. "I have to make a quick run," I said, kissing her on the lips. She was nervous and didn't want me to leave, but there were things that could not be undone. I had to go.

"Please, just make sure you come back to me," Summer said, sitting on the bed. "I'll be back. I promise," I said, walking out of the room.

Northeast Philadelphia

Victor's rigid snores could be heard throughout his large home. Peacefully asleep, he never heard the front door quickly open and close. Walking upstairs into his bedroom, Prince stood over Victor's body holding the loaded 45 chrome berretta.

"Wake the FUCK UP!!!" Prince said, smacking Victor awake from the peaceful dream he was having. "WHOA!!! Prince!!! What...how?" Victor said, sitting up with his hands on his face in complete shock.

"How did you get in here?" Victor asked. "Alexander let me in," Prince said, showing Victor the keys to the front door.

"Prince, look…,"

"Shut up, Victor! You tried to kill me, motherfucker! You sent Alexander to kill me!" Prince yelled. "Why Victor?" he continued.

"Prince, you were leaving me, my friend. You know too much. Way too much!" Victor said. "We couldn't take that chance!"

"Victor, I would have never crossed you. Never!"

"I just couldn't take that chance, Prince. And neither could Alexander. That's why he never liked you because he couldn't trust you. If you ever decided to quit and leave us, you could have a lot of heat on us."

"I was your friend, Victor!"

"You still are, Prince, remember who helped you get out of prison? It was me. I'm the one who was there for you when everyone else left you. I saved your life, Prince!"

"No, Victor, you changed my life! You turned me into someone I didn't want to be," Prince said, as all of his victims' faces flashed in his eyes.

"Please, Prince! Please don't kill me! I have money in the closet. Take it. Take it! I have property and so many things I could give you! Please, let's' fix this," Victor pleaded. Looking into Victor's eyes, Prince saw the same fear that he had seen in all of the men's eyes he had killed.

"I'm sorry, Victor, but I can't take that chance. You know too much," Prince said, pulling the trigger and shooting Victor once in the head.

Victor's blood started to cover his bed sheets as his lifeless body slumped into the bed. Prince then walked over to the closet and opened it. Inside was a large, beautifully decorated brown wooden box that was filled with money.

Prince removed one-hundred-thousand dollars to cover the cost of the four men that he had killed in South Beach and an additional twenty-five thousand for Victor. Now they were truly even.

CHAPTER 23

"Where did you go?" Summer said, laying her beautiful light honey brown body across the bed. "I had to take care of one last problem," Prince said, getting undressed.

"Is everything okay now?" she asked. "Everything is fine now. Couldn't be better," Prince said, joining Summer on the bed.

Looking on his walls, Prince noticed that the "Pain" portrait had been removed.

"Where's Pain?" he asked Summer. "I took it down and threw it away. You don't need that anymore," Summer smiled. Looking into Summer's eyes, Prince said, "Thank you," as a tear fell from his eye. "Thank you," he said, as he became overwhelmed with emotion and held Summer tightly in his arms; thanking God for sparing their lives.

One Year Later

The sun beamed down hard on this beautiful hot summer day. Sitting outside of the beach house villa on the exotic island of Jamaica, Summer lay across Prince's lap.

The heat reminded her of one of the deadliest summers she had endured, and Summer was thankful she survived it. Philadelphia had been her home but after losing her father, her uncle, her best friend Keisha, an unborn sibling; and almost losing her life and her lover, Prince, Summer could no longer call the City of Brotherly Love her home.

Summer and Prince discussed places to call home. They thought long and hard and finally came to an agreement.

Sonny's passing ensured that Summer would never have to work again. The million dollar life insurance policy was hers, as well as all of his properties; and the money he had in his safe and his bank accounts. She had full financial freedom and nothing to keep her in Philly.

Summer sold her house in Wynnefield, her father's barbershop, bar and three apartment buildings. Then she gave her beauty salon and the apartments within to Latoya. It was difficult to leave her friend, Latoya; however Nolan, Earl, and Latoya had an open invitation to visit her whenever they wanted to. Now that Summer and Prince were permanent residents of the island, Jamaica was always a great place for their friends to come and visit them.

Hearing the sound of a vigorous crying baby, Summer quickly sat up. "It's your turn, Daddy," she said, smiling as Prince stood up and walked inside the house. A few moments later, Prince returned and sat back down next to his beautiful wife.

"Who was it this time?" Summer said, lying back across Prince's lap. "Lil Sonny's pacifier came out of his mouth again, but I put it back in, and he's going back to sleep. And Keisha is still sound asleep. Nothing wakes up sleepy beauty," Prince said, talking about their newborn twins.

Looking out at the bright yellow sun, the gorgeous blue Atlantic Ocean and crystal white sand, Prince turned and looked into Summer's beautiful glowing face.

"So how's my light shining?" Prince said as he began running his hand through Summer's hair. "As bright as ever, knowing I'll always have you."

We want to send a heartfelt thank you to our readers.
We enjoy this work we are blessed to do and are
hopeful you'll continue to take this journey with us!

Tiona & Jimmy

Black Scarface

Black Scarface II

Black Scarface III

Black Scarface IV

DOC

King

Contract Killer

Killadelphia

On Everything I Love

Money Desires & Regrets

What Every Woman Wants

Young Rich & Dangerous

The Underworld

A Rose Among Thorns

A Rose Among Thorns 2

Sex Slave

WE SHIP TO PRISONS

| Ain't No Sunshine | WHO? | The Darkest Corner | Hottest Summer Ever |

Place Your Order Now & Thank You For Your Continued Support!

Jimmy DaSaint

COMING SOON

| KING II | Black Gotti | The Crew | The Rise of A Dynasty |

DASAINT ENTERTAINMENT ORDER FORM

Please visit www.dasaintentertainment.com to place online orders.

You can also fill out this form and send it to:

DASAINT ENTERTAINMENT
PO BOX 97
BALA CYNWYD, PA 19004

TITLE	PRICE	QTY
BLACK SCARFACE	$15.00	_____
BLACK SCARFACE II	$15.00	_____
BLACK SCARFACE III	$15.00	_____
BLACK SCARFACE IV	$15.00	_____
DOC	$15.00	_____
KING	$15.00	_____
CONTRACT KILLER	$15.00	_____
KILLADELPHIA	$15.00	_____
ON EVERYTHING I LOVE	$15.00	_____
MONEY DESIRES & REGRETS	$15.00	_____
WHAT EVERY WOMAN WANTS	$15.00	_____
YOUNG RICH & DANGEROUS	$15.00	_____
THE UNDERWORLD	$15.00	_____
A ROSE AMONG THORNS	$15.00	_____
A ROSE AMONG THORNS II	$15.00	_____
SEX SLAVE	$15.00	_____
AIN'T NO SUNSHINE	$15.00	_____
WHO	$15.00	_____
THE DARKEST CORNER	$15.00	_____
HOTTEST SUMMER EVER	$15.00	_____

Make Checks or Money Orders payable to:
DASAINT ENTERTAINMENT

NAME: _____

ADDRESS: _____

_____

CITY: _____ STATE: _____ ZIP:_____

PHONE:_____

PRISON ID NUMBER_____

$3.50 per item for Shipping and Handling
($4.95 per item for Expedited Shipping)

PO BOX 97
BALA CYNWYD, PA 19004
WWW.DASAINTENTERTAINMENT.COM

WANTED :
AUTHORS

Authors if you are interested in a potential Publishing Contract with DaSaint Entertainment, please be sure to read this carefully.

Submit a synopsis of your work, along with the first four chapters of your book, and a reading submission fee of fifty dollars to:
DaSaint Entertainment, PO Box 97, Bala Cynwyd PA 19004.
No submissions will be accepted without the required fees.
Money orders only-made out to: DaSaint Entertainment.
Send copies because your material will not be returned!

Due to the volume of entries, you will be contacted within six months of your postmarked submissions. Should your entry be chosen, you will be given further instructions and will become a part of the DaSaint Entertainment Family.

Note:
- All work must be the author's original material. No plagiarized works will be accepted!
- You can not be under contract with any other publishing house, and the work you submit must not have been published before.
- DaSaint Entertainment reserves the right to refuse any works based on their professional evaluation.

We look forward to reviewing your work!
DaSaint Entertainment

Made in the USA
Coppell, TX
14 March 2022

74959269R00115